BILLY SURE

KID ENTREPRENEUR

AND THE **NO-TROUBLE BUBBLE**

INVENTED BY **LUKE SHARPE**

DRAWINGS BY **GRAHAM ROSS**

Simon Spotlight

New York   London   Toronto   Sydney   New Delhi

SIMON SPOTLIGHT

An imprint of Simon & Schuster Children's Publishing Division

1230 Avenue of the Americas, New York, New York 10020

This Simon Spotlight edition January 2016

Copyright © 2016 by Simon & Schuster, Inc. Text by Michael Teitelbaum. Illustrations by Graham Ross. All rights reserved, including the right of reproduction in whole or in part in any form.

SIMON SPOTLIGHT and colophon are registered trademarks of Simon & Schuster, Inc.

For information about special discounts for bulk purchases, please contact Simon & Schuster Special Sales at 1-866-506-1949 or business@simonandschuster.com.

Designed by Jay Colvin

The text of this book was set in Minya Nouvelle.

Manufactured in the United States of America 1215 FFG

10 9 8 7 6 5 4 3 2 1

ISBN 978-1-4814-5275-5 (hc)

ISBN 978-1-4814-5274-8 (pbk)

ISBN 978-1-4814-5276-2 (eBook)

Library of Congress Control Number 2015933267

Chapter One

The Next "Next Big Thing"

MY NAME IS BILLY SURE. I'M AN INVENTOR. MY company, **SURE THINGS, INC.,** has come out with all kinds of stuff, ranging from the **ALL BALL**—our first product which is a ball that can transform into different kinds of sports balls—to our latest product, **GROSS-TO-GOOD POWDER.** It makes anything—and I mean *anything*, even frog legs wrapped in stinky cheese—taste good.

Okay, full disclosure. Credit for a lot of the development for the Gross-to-Good Powder goes to my big sister, Emily. She's fourteen.

When Sure Things, Inc. began, few people could have shown less interest than Emily did, either in me or in my activities, even when those activities included starting a SUCCESSFUL BUSINESS at age twelve.

But something has started to change between Emily and me recently. Oh, don't get me wrong. It's not like a "we've become best buds, let's hang out, you're my favorite person in the world" kind of change. It's more like an "I no longer wish you lived on another planet" kind of change.

Let me explain. I go to Fillmore Middle

School, where I'm in seventh grade. I'm also the president of the Fillmore Inventors Club. I help students with ideas for inventions. It adds one more thing to my ridiculously busy life—school, running a business, homework, spending time with my dad and my dog, Philo—you get the idea. But with this club, I really have helped kids develop their ideas, and even more importantly, have helped to give them a place where they feel they belong.

But I'm getting off topic, which is something I do a lot!

Not long ago, the inventors club had been trying—unsuccessfully—to come up with a way to make spinach taste good. Then Emily showed up unexpectedly at a club meeting with a powder she had created that actually worked. Sprinkle a little of Emily's powder on your spinach, and spinach is no longer to be feared! But then we had the idea to expand the powder's powers. Together, Emily, Manny, and I tweaked her invention to make it work so that *everything* you sprinkle it on tastes good.

But who's Manny, you might ask?

Manny's my business partner in Sure Things, Inc. And I do mean *business* partner. Manny handles the marketing, packaging, advertising, getting people to invest in our products, and on and on. If it has to do with numbers or selling, Manny is all over it.

He's also my best friend, which he was long before Sure Things, Inc. came about.

Anyway, since Emily's help with the now WILDLY SUCCESSFUL Gross-to-Good Powder, she's shown much more interest in the company, and we're getting along better than we ever have.

Today, Emily has joined Manny and me in the Sure Things, Inc. office, located in the garage at Manny's house. She doesn't come here often. In fact, until she came up with her powder not long ago, she had never actually bothered to step inside. I'm at my workbench, a.k.a. the Mad Scientist Division of Sure Things, Inc., cleaning up a bit following the frenzy—and mess—that always happens when I'm in the throes of inventing. And by "cleaning up," I mean shoving piles of wires, switches, bulbs, knobs, and a rainbow-colored wig (don't ask) off my worktable into a nearby drawer. Which leaves only about four layers of stuff on top of the table.

Manny is hunched over his keyboard, as usual, tracking up-to-the-minute sales figures on all of our products.

Emily is sitting next to me. Every time she looks at the mess on my workbench, she shakes her head and turns away.

"What's the latest on the Gross-to-Good Powder?" Emily asks Manny.

Manny continues to tap away on the keyboard.

"Uh, Manny," Emily continues, "when someone asks you a question, the polite thing to do is to answer it. At least that's how it works with NORMAL HUMANS."

Okay, so maybe Emily doesn't want to ship *me* off to Saturn anymore, but I can't say the same for my best friend. . . .

Manny whirls around in his chair to face us.

"Numbers are great. The Midwest is leading the way with a forty-seven percent rise in sales over the last three weeks," he reports.

"I would have thought that our house was leading the way, since we put the powder on every single thing Dad cooks!" Emily jokes.

I love my dad. He's a great artist and gardener, but he is, hands down, the world's worst cook. Dad wasn't always the only family chef. My mom travels a lot as a scientist doing research for the government, and about nine months ago she left for her longest trip yet. She wasn't much better at cooking either, but Mom loved to order in pizza. Dad? Well, Dad likes pizza, but with his own additions. Asparagus, kale, codfish, chia seeds, stinky cheese instead of regular cheese . . . Dad's cooking is really gross.

Only he doesn't think so. Fortunately, Emily filled our salt shaker at home with the Gross-to-Good Powder, so now Dad can keep thinking he's a great cook, we don't have to hurt his feelings by telling him otherwise, and we can stand to eat his cooking every night.

As for my mom, I miss her a lot, although we e-mail all the time and video chat when possible.

And so, at least for the time being, Emily and I have one of Dad's bizarre concoctions to look forward to each night at dinnertime. In fact, Dad is so proud of his cooking that his latest painting project is a series of still lifes based on the strange dishes he's come up with. It's a little weird. I mean, who would want to buy a painting of JELLIED TUNA?

"That's fantastic, Manny," I say after hearing the rundown of our sales figures.

"Absolutely," replies Manny. Then, without missing a beat, "So, what's next?"

That's my partner. As soon as one invention is selling like crazy, Manny is ready to jump into what we're going to do next.

"I have a file of ideas we've rejected," I say. "Maybe we could rethink one of those." I grab a cardboard file box out from under my desk and pull off the lid. Okay—maybe I'm

not the most organized. The file has rejected
inventions in it, but it's also got doodles of
my favorite baseball team, the Hyenas, and
the math homework I forgot to hand in last
week.

"Let's see . . . there's the pen that turns into
a jet pack . . ." I begin, reading off the correct paper. "Nah, getting the engine that small
could take years."

"What about another product like the
SIBLING SILENCER?" Emily asks. She
smiles smugly. Emily loves using Sure Things,
Inc.'s second product on me. Last week
she silenced me when I was talking
about superheroes. Just as I was about
to tell her about how I'd love to be
invisible, **ZING!** I couldn't talk any

more. Note to self: Install a "Billy Immunity" option on future models.

"Actually, I didn't invent that," I say. "That came out of our Next Big Thing contest where other young inventors submitted their ideas on our website. We picked the one we liked the best and helped the inventor make it a reality."

"So, why not do that again?" asks Emily.

I turn to Manny, who seems to be half listening and half answering his e-mails, even though he's the one who started this conversation.

"What do you think, Manny?" I ask.

Manny doesn't react. Make that one-quarter listening, and three-quarters answering e-mails.

"I don't think he heard you, Billy," says Emily. "Working with someone like this every day would drive me—"

"What if we took the contest ONE STEP FURTHER?" Manny says suddenly, turning to look right at us. "What if we turned the Next Big Thing contest into a TV show?"

Emily shoots me a look that I can only

interpret as: Okay, maybe working with this guy is not so bad after all.

"A TV show?" I ask.

"Yeah. Well, more like a TV show special, where young inventors present everything from rough ideas to preliminary sketches to first-pass prototypes. Then the judges—I'm thinking the three of us—vote. It won't be about who has already made the best invention, but who has the best idea. Just like with the Sibling Silencer, the winning inventor would share in the profits, and the TV show would be marketing in itself!"

"That would be way cooler than just sending your idea to a website," says Emily.

"But how do we even do that?" I ask. "I mean, a TV show? Where do we start?"

"I'll get in touch with Chris Fernell," Manny says. "He should be able to point us in the right direction."

Chris Fernell is the host of **Better Than Sleeping!**, the TV show where I was interviewed just after the All Ball hit big. He's somewhat of a friend, or as much of a friend as a TV host can be with a kid, and that's pretty cool.

"This is fantastic," I say. "Doing a TV show again, *and* helping a young inventor, *and* coming up with Sure Things' NEXT BIG THING! Wow!"

As usual, Manny has the answer. Reason #988 why I'm glad that he's my best friend and my business partner.

Chapter Two

The Game Plan

I'LL BE HONEST. THERE'S MORE THAN ONE REASON I'M excited about the TV show contest.

You see, my BIRTHDAY is coming up—March 28. In the past, I've had awesome birthday parties: ice skating, laser tag, the movies, more laser tag, you name it. But this year I've been so busy that I haven't had time to plan anything. And if I turn thirteen all by myself with only Philo for company . . . well, that would be really *ruff*. (See what I did there?) But with the TV show, I might have time to start thinking about what to do on my big day, since I won't be busy inventing.

The next morning before school I shoot off a quick e-mail to my mom. Mom always knows how to cheer me up. Like I said, I really do miss her. One thing that's helped a bit is that we've started to have more video chats. Seeing her face always makes me feel better.

I plop myself down at my computer, rub the gunk out of my eyes, and type:

Hi Mom,

I wanted to catch up, so here goes! The Gross-to-Good Powder—the stuff that Emily helped us invent that makes even Dad's cooking taste good—is doing really well. I guess Dad's not the only terrible cook in the world.

Are you ready for a shocker? Emily has been stopping by the office. She actually seems interested in what we're doing there. It's kinda cool, although sometimes I wonder if spies have kidnapped her and replaced her with a robot double who's been programmed to be nice to me.

The really, really exciting news is that Manny is trying to set up a TV show for us so we can hold a contest to help pick Sure Things' Next Big Thing. Which means I might get to be on TV again! If anyone can set this up, it's Manny. Anyway, gotta get to school. Do you have time for a video chat tonight?

Love you,

Billy

I hit send, then hurry off.

After a pretty uneventful day at school, I scoot home, grab a snack, pick up Philo, and head to the office. I walk through the door to find Manny on the phone. It doesn't take me long to figure out who he is talking to.

"That's right, we would be the judges . . . what? I guess we could get some other judges if you think that would be better . . . a big name, huh?"

A BIG NAME? On our show? Who would

14

we ask? I start to think about the celebrities we could invite . . . Dustin Peeler, the pop star, is a big fan of the All Ball, but he's gone off the grid lately. Gemma Weston? She's an actress-turned-humanitarian who was caught using the Gross-to-Good Powder at a restaurant last week. As I said before, our inventions are pretty popular. Hmm.

"So if we get him, you're on to produce? Deal? Deal! Thanks, Chris. I'll be back to you in a flash. Later, babe."

Manny hangs up.

"'Back to you in a flash'? 'Later, babe'? Don't tell me you've gone all Hollywood on me now," I say, unable to hold back a smile.

"You gotta speak their language, Billy," Manny says, trying to sound serious but fighting back a smile. "So here's the deal. Chris Fernell loves the idea of doing a TV show to help pick our Next Big Thing."

"I can't believe it's that easy."

"It isn't."

"Oh." It never is.

"He loves the idea and has even agreed to produce the show himself, through his production company, **Big Time TV**," Manny continues.

"I hear a big fat 'but' coming up," I say.

"Here it is," says Manny. "Chris will produce the show, but only if we can get a big-name sponsor to be our partner and participate.

"Chris suggested reaching out to Carl Bourette and the Hyenas baseball team! He remembered how excited both you and Carl were to meet each other when you appeared on his show. What do you think?"

Okay, that's a way better idea than Gemma Weston! I've been a fan of Carl Bourette's since his rookie year. I even have his rookie trading

card. It was an amazing thrill to meet him when we were both on **Better Than Sleeping!** And the weird thing about that was that Carl was as excited to meet me as I was to meet him. Turns out Carl and his Hyenas teammates are big fans of the All Ball!

"Are you kidding?" I say, practically jumping out of my skin. "A chance to see Carl Bourette again, much less work with him on a TV show? Nah, I think I'll pass."

Manny's eyes open wide.

"GOTCHA!" I say. "Of course I want to do this!"

"I'll call the Hyenas' office and see what

we can work out," Manny says, smiling. But I smile bigger.

"I have a better idea," I say, pointing to the bulletin board above my workbench. Every square inch is covered with papers, sketches, photos, napkins I've scribbled on . . . you get the idea. But prominently displayed, right in the center of this ever-changing collage, is a printed copy of the Hyenas' baseball schedule. "The Hyenas have a preseason game this afternoon. Why don't we go and see if we can talk to Carl in person?"

"Play ball," says Manny, closing his laptop and heading for the door.

"Three tickets, please," I say, stepping up to the window at Hyenas Stadium. Manny's dad agreed to take us to the ballpark on super-short notice. I can feel my excitement building. I always get happy when I see a baseball game, and today I have the added excitement of seeing Carl Bourette, and maybe getting the chance to work with him again.

The stadium is a beautiful sight. I smile when I get my first glance at the field. As busy as my life is, I have got to find a way to go to more Hyenas games.

Before we sit down, Manny and his dad head to a food stand. They're not nearly as big baseball fans as I am, even though they are always willing to join me at a game. I actually think that Manny's favorite part of the game is the food. The three of us share a tray filled with four giant hot dogs, a mountain of fries, and two large sodas.

Yup, it's definitely the food.

As I munch on a hot dog, a voice booms from the stadium's loudspeaker:

"Ladies and gentlemen, welcome to Hyenas Stadium for today's game between the Mighty Oaks and your hometown heroes, the Hyenas!"

A roar goes up from the crowd.

"And now . . . it's time . . . to PLAY BALL!"

With that, the Hyenas take the field.

"**THERE'S CARL!**" I shout, pointing to the player running out to take his position at shortstop.

The game begins. I settle into the easy rhythm of pitches, hits, strikeouts, walks, and the rest. Manny jumps out of his seat . . . on his way toward his third hot dog.

The game is close and exciting. When the top of the ninth inning rolls around, the Hyenas trail 2-3, and things look like they are about to get worse for the home team. The Oaks have the bases loaded with two outs. And to make matters worse, their best hitter strides to the plate.

A nervous buzz passes through the crowd, shifting to the ever-familiar chant of:

"Let's go Hyenas, ha, ha, HA!"

The Hyenas' pitcher goes into his motion just as Manny returns with another hot dog. The pitcher delivers his pitch.

The batter swings and smacks a sharply hit ground ball toward short. Carl hustles to his right, slides onto the outfield grass, and makes a backhanded grab of the ball. Popping back up to his feet, Carl turns and fires the ball across the diamond. It slams into the first baseman's mitt with a loud *crack!*

The umpire signals that the batter is out. The crowd cheers wildly as the Hyenas trot toward their dugout.

"Yeah, Carl!" I shout. "What a fantastic play," I say to Manny, who nods and mumbles through his full mouth.

Bottom of the ninth. The Hyenas' catcher leads off. Carl steps into the on-deck circle. He'll be batting second this inning. The Hyenas have to score, or they'll lose the game.

The Hyenas' catcher lines the first pitch into left field for a single. Carl walks up to the plate.

"Come on, Carl, end this game!" I shout.

Carl measures out his swing. The first pitch is outside. Ball one. The next pitch flies right down the middle of the plate. Carl swings and drives the ball deep to right field . . . going . . . going . . . GONE! A two-run, walk-off, game-winning home run!

The crowd stands and cheers as Carl trots around the bases. His teammates are all at home plate jumping up and down.

"What a game!" I say as we head from our seats.

"Now we can talk to Carl about the TV show," says Manny, letting out an enormous belch.

We wind our way down to the lower level of the stadium, eventually coming to the Hyenas' locker room. A security guard blocks the door.

"Hi, boys. If you're looking for autographs, you'll have to wait outside," the guard explains.

"Actually, we're here to talk with Carl Bourette about a business proposition," Manny says in his most matter-of-fact tone.

"Really?" the guard says, raising his eyebrows skeptically.

I pull a Sure Things, Inc. business card out of my pocket and hand it over. "If you could please give this to Carl and say that Billy Sure

SURE THINGS, INC.
Very Official
Business

would like to speak with him, that would be great," I say.

"Wait here," says the guard, who turns and disappears into the locker room.

A few seconds later he returns, followed by Carl Bourette! He is still in his dirty uniform, but I'm so excited I don't care.

"Hey, it's my old pal!" Carl says, shaking my hand. He turns to the guard. "It's okay, Frank. I'm a big fan of Billy Sure. Come on in, boys."

I follow Carl into the locker room. I can't believe I'm inside the Hyenas' locker room! How cool is this? Manny trails along behind me.

Manny! Oh, gee, he shouldn't be *behind* me! We're business partners. That means side by side.

"Carl, you remember my business partner, Manny," I say.

Carl turns around and starts to reach his hand out to shake Manny's, when three of his teammates surround me.

"Billy Sure!" says one player.

"Hey! It's Mr. All Ball!" shouts another.

"We love that thing!" adds another. "You're the greatest!"

"Well, actually, it's not all me," I begin. "My partner—"

Carl puts his arm around my shoulder. "Guys, this is my buddy Billy Sure," he says to his teammates.

I look back and see Manny standing there, staring at his shoes. I start to feel bad about everyone focusing on me. Sure Things, Inc. would not exist without Manny.

"And this is Manny Reyes," I say, gesturing behind me. "My partner at Sure Things—"

"HEY, BILLY, CATCH!" calls a voice from across the locker room, interrupting me.

I turn toward the voice just in time to see a Hyenas player softly tossing a hockey puck toward me. As soon as it leaves his hand, it changes into a baseball.

"The All Ball rules!" shouts the player as I catch the baseball.

"So what did you want to talk to me about?" asks Carl. We all sit down on benches. Me, sitting on a bench in the Hyenas' locker room! Wow!

Anyway, finally, down to business. And finally, Manny can take part in the conversation.

"We've been talking to Chris Fernell from **Better Than Sleeping!** about doing a TV show," I explain. "A contest for young inventors. Manny, my sister Emily, and I are going to be the judges."

"Whoever wins will get Sure Things, Inc.'s help in turning their idea into a real product," Manny adds.

"Sounds fantastic," says Carl. "But where do I come in?"

"Oh yeah," I say. "Chris will only agree to produce the show if we can get a big-name sponsor to be our partner."

"As a matter of fact, Chris is the one who

suggested we get in touch with you to see if you and the Hyenas would like to be part of this," says Manny.

Carl looks right at me. "Do a TV show with you?" he says. "Sounds great! Let me check with our management, and I'll let you know."

Carl stands up. "Gotta grab a shower and get out of here, but great to see you, Billy," he says, shaking my hand.

What about Manny?

Carl reaches out and shakes Manny's hand. Phew. "Nice to see you again, Manny."

"You too, Carl," Manny says.

Manny and I head out of the locker room and to the parking lot.

"Even if nothing comes of this, I got to see Carl again and visit the Hyenas' locker room," I say, still feeling ON TOP OF THE WORLD. "What a great day."

"And I got to eat four ballpark hot dogs," Manny adds, smiling. "A really great day!" Then he belches again, even louder than the first time.

Chapter Three

From Babe Ruth to See Ya, Babe

I ARRIVE HOME IN A GREAT MOOD, WHICH IS ONLY made better when I find an e-mail from my mom saying that she is available for a video chat this evening. As a matter of fact—I check my watch—in fifteen minutes!

I grab an energy bar and a glass of juice and settle into my favorite chair, set up the video chat window on my laptop, and wait for Mom's face to appear. A few moments later, there she is.

"Hi, honey! I'm so happy to see you," she says.

She appears to be in a hotel room somewhere.

"Me too, Mom. Where are you?"

"Oh, nowhere important. How's that TV show coming?"

As usual, Mom doesn't seem to want to tell me where she is. Oh well. There's more important stuff on my mind. "The TV show idea is moving along. The producers want a big name involved and suggested Carl Bourette!"

"How exciting!" says Mom. "So is he going to be on your TV show?"

"Not sure yet, but I hope so."

And then I tell Mom what's been on my mind a lot lately. "So, you know my birthday is coming up soon, right?"

"Of course."

"And I'm turning thirteen, which means I'm about to become a TEENAGER."

"You did that math all by yourself, huh?" Mom jokes. "It's hard for me to believe that I'm about to have two teenagers. I can't wait to see you and give you a big birthday hug."

"Funny you should say that. I would really, really love for you to come home for my birthday," I admit. I'm not sure if I have time to plan a whole birthday party. So if I can't have that, I want to spend the day with Mom.

"Oh, Billy," she says.

I know it's serious when she calls me "Billy" instead of "honey."

"I'm right in the middle of a huge project. I don't think I can get there for your birthday. I'm so sorry. I feel terrible."

"Well, if there's any way you can, that would be fantastic."

"You'll be the first to know, honey," she says, but I know it's hopeless.

A couple of minutes later she signs off and I'm staring at a blank screen, wishing my mom could be home for my big birthday.

The next morning, I come downstairs for breakfast to discover Dad making a concoction of pickle-and-pineapple waffles. I'm used to Dad's wacky food combinations, but when he *thwaps!* on homemade avocado-licorice syrup, I decide this might be his all-time weirdest.

Once again, I'm grateful to Emily for getting the ball rolling on the Gross-to-Good Powder. I grab the salt shaker—which is now always filled with the powder at our house—sprinkle some onto my green-tinted waffles, and dig in.

"Good waffles, Dad," I'm able to say without lying.

"It must be my SECRET INGREDIENT," Dad says.

"You mean the pickles?" I ask.

"No, the fish oil," Dad says, and then digs in to his ginormous stack.

BLECH!

A couple of minutes later Emily comes downstairs. I immediately notice that the long purple braid she's had for the past few weeks is gone, but I don't say anything. No matter how well we've been getting along lately, I know better than to ask Emily about what she is or isn't wearing, or any hairstyle, eyewear, or method of speaking. These can all change without warning with the old thing forgotten and the new thing being the most important thing she's ever done.

On first glance I can't figure out what her new "thing" might be. Is it possible she's out-grown having to have a new "thing"?

"Have some of my secret-ingredient waffles," Dad says, as Emily takes a seat at the table.

Emily immediately reaches for the salt shaker. As she grabs it, I hear a loud clinking noise. That's when I see that she has a funky ring on each of her ten fingers. Some have col-ored stones on them. One is a gold butterfly. Another is a silver skull.

This must be her next new "thing." Ignore, I tell myself. Ignore.

"So, Dad, it looks like Manny, Emily, and I might be doing a TV show with Chris Fernell to help us find our next invention," I say.

Emily tries to pick up her knife. It clatters against her rings and drops back onto the table. She tries the fork instead. That she manages to grasp awkwardly in her palm as if it were a weapon. She attacks her waffles. *Hi-yaaaaa!*

"That's fantastic!" says Dad, eyeing Emily's antics but looking away quickly, knowing full well what staring or, worse yet, commenting would bring.

"Oh, I also had a video chat with Mom last night," I continue. "I told her how much I miss her and also how much I wish she could be here for my birthday. You know, it being a big one and all."

"What a great idea!" says Dad.

"Yeah, well, it doesn't sound like Mom can make it." Saying it aloud makes me realize just how much I want Mom to be here for my birthday.

Ka-Rash!!!!

The sound of glass shattering pulls me out of my gloomy thoughts. It seems that Emily grabbed a glass of OJ with her fully armored fingers, smashing the glass to bits. Luckily, she isn't hurt. I can't say the same for the glass.

"Sorry, Dad," she says, jumping up from the table to grab a sponge.

"I can get you a straw, if you like," I say. "You know, that way you don't have to touch any glasses with your rings."

Uh-oh. It kinda just slipped out.

"What do you know about anything?" Emily snaps, as she sops up the spilled juice with a sponge and wipes the pieces of glass into a garbage can. "You're just a clueless twelve-year-old!"

I'm about to point out that I am almost thirteen, but then I think better of it. I go back to my waffles.

I arrive at the office that afternoon with Philo in tow. I'm glad that Emily is on board to be one of the judges, but how she'll be able to hold a pencil to write down her scores is beyond me.

As I start to jot down ideas for how the TV show might go, the feeling of missing my mom starts to sour my mood. My mom and I have always been close. She used to drive Manny and me to school. Which reminds me . . . Manny! Manny was my best friend long before he was my business partner. I decide to talk to him about it.

"So you know my birthday's coming up soon," I say.

"Uhh . . . of course," Manny says slowly, almost like he forgot.

"I asked my mom if she can come home, but she said she can't make it. I'm really bummed," I say.

Manny turns toward me.

"I'm sure she'd be here if she could," he says. "Maybe you could do a video chat with her on that day."

Not a bad idea. A poor substitute for having her here, but better than nothing.

Before I can say anything, Manny's phone rings.

"It's Chris," he says, reading the caller ID. "I'll put the call on speaker. Here we go. . . ."

A voice BOOMS out of Manny's speaker.

"Manny! It's Chris Fernell, Big Time TV. How are ya, babe?"

"Good, Chris. Listen, I've got Billy here to join us on the confab."

Join us on the confab? Sometimes I don't understand Manny at all.

"Billy Sure, kid entrepreneur . . . How are ya, babe?"

I try hard not to roll my eyes.

"Hi, Chris," I say. Somehow just saying "hi" feels boring. Like I'm a foreigner who just arrived in the land of Show Biz.

"Good news, fellas," Chris continues. "The

Billy Sure
Show Biz
tourist!

Hyenas have agreed to cosponsor the TV show, and even to brand the winning product with their team logo!"

"I'm lovin' it, Chris!" says Manny, winking at me to let me know that he, too, realizes that this is all one big game. Manny happens to be good at the game. I am not.

"But here's the thing, Manny, babe. The Hyenas are insisting that Carl Bourette be one of the judges. I think that's a fabulous idea, don't you?"

Manny and I look at each other. I shrug. Why not?

"Fabulous doesn't even begin to describe it, Chris," says Manny.

"Oh, and my partners here at Big Time TV think we should have five judges," Chris went on. "It's a nice odd number. And five people always looks good on TV."

With Manny, me, Emily, and Carl, we have four. Maybe Gemma Weston isn't out of the judges' circle after all? But somehow that just doesn't feel right. I smile. I know *exactly* who should be our fifth judge!

"What about ABBY NIELSON?" I ask. "She's the inventor who won our first contest, the one we ran through our website. She came up with the idea for the Sibling Silencer. She'd be really inspiring to the inventors."

"I love it!" says Chris. "Any other brilliant ideas?"

I look at Manny. I realize now that aside from the Hollywood lingo, he hasn't said much on the phone call. I feel some regret in my stomach. I should have probably run the Abby idea by him first.

"Any ideas, Manny?" I say, repeating Chris Fernell's question.

He thinks about it for a second. Then, in his ever-professional Manny way, says, "Let's make the show a two-part special. That would build excitement and ratings, and maximize ad dollars. The first night can be an elimination round. The six best ideas according to the judges will move into the finals on the second night. That night we'll pick the one winner whose invention will become the Next Big Thing."

Two-part special? DOUBLE the TV time?

"I love it!" Chris says. "Let's continue this confab later. Gotta fly . . . meetings, meetings, meetings. Bye, babe!"

And so our confab ends.

"Are you gonna talk like that until the TV show is done, babe?" I ask Manny. "Or should I say, TV *shows*."

After that, I shoot off a quick e-mail to Abby, hoping she'll agree to be a judge. Then I leave the office in a pretty good mood. But the closer I get to home, the more my thoughts turn back to my birthday and Mom.

Chapter Four

Meet the Judges

WHEN I CHECK MY E-MAIL THE NEXT MORNING I see that Abby has replied.

> Hi Billy,
> So nice to hear from you. And thank you for thinking of me for your TV show! I would be thrilled and honored to be a judge. Count me in!
> —Abby

Good news. I immediately e-mail Manny to let him know that we have our five judges. I get a reply from him, telling me that he has already set up a meeting for this Saturday morning with Chris and the five judges—something he obviously did before we even knew if we had five judges. Oh-so-Manny.

I reply to Abby, forwarding the details. I'm starting to get excited about this TV show, and about all the ideas that we'll be seeing, one of which will be our Next Big Thing.

I take advantage of my good mood to write to Mom. I let her know that the TV show is a go and it's going to be a lot of fun. It's a pretty upbeat e-mail, but I can't resist reminding her how much I wish she could be here for my birthday. I take Manny's advice and ask her to make time for a video chat on that day.

The next few days at the office are filled with brainstorming discussions and outlines, trying to be as prepared as possible before our big meeting. Manny has to reign himself in to avoid developing marketing plans for a product we haven't even seen the idea for yet. I come up with a scoring system for the judges that is fair.

The system works like this: Each judge gives between one and five points in five categories—ORIGINALITY, CREATIVITY, USEFULNESS, MARKETABILITY, and EASE OF MANUFACTURING. We then total the scores at the end of the show to figure out the winner.

When Saturday morning rolls around, Emily and I climb into Dad's car.

"Big day, guys," says Dad, never one to miss an opportunity for understatement.

A few minutes later we pull up at Manny's house. He climbs in.

"Hi, Mr. Sure," he says. "Thanks for the ride."

"Anything for our budding TV stars!" replies Dad.

After a forty-five-minute ride we arrive downtown. Dad pulls into the parking lot of the TV station where we'll be filming the special. Chris Fernell has flown in from Los Angeles to be here. I can see Emily twist her rings on her fingers. I'm not totally sure about what my sister is thinking, but I think she twists those rings when she's nervous.

That's when a bright yellow, super-cool convertible sports car comes speeding into the parking lot. It glides to a stop in the parking space next to us, and out steps Carl Bourette. Next to Carl's car, Dad's sensible car looks like a tricycle.

"Good morning, Billy!" says Carl.

"Hi, Carl," I say, still somewhat in a state of disbelief that I am on a first-name basis with Carl Bourette.

"Hey, guys," Carl says, extending his hand. He shakes Manny's hand. Then he shakes Emily's hand. The expression on his face tells me that he is puzzled by her rings, but Carl must be smart, too, because he doesn't say anything.

"Big fan!" Dad says, smiling broadly as he shakes Carl's hand. "I was there when you hit that grand slam in the All-Star game a few years back. That was something!"

"Thank you," says Carl. "Well, I think you've got an all-star right here. An ALL-STAR INVENTOR, that is!"

I can see Emily's eyes rolling without even looking.

As we head toward the front door, a station wagon pulls into the parking lot. Out comes a girl with a woman that I assume is her mom.

"Hi, I'm Abby Nielson," says the girl.

"Abby!" I say, walking over to her. It's at that moment I realize that not only haven't we ever met, but I forgot what Abby looks like. Yes, she sent me a video demonstration of the Sibling Silencer, but that was way back at the beginning of the school year. She's cute in that friendly kind of way, with short dark hair and big black-rimmed glasses that just scream out "HIP NERD."

We shake hands.

"And you must be Manny," says Abby, turning to him. "I loved the paper you posted last week about RAM efficiency. That rocked!"

Wow! She speaks tech geek like Manny, but she's also a creative inventor. Kinda like a cross between the two of us.

"Thanks," Manny says. That's when I notice something weird. Is he blushing?

"And this is my sister, Emily," I say.

Abby shakes Emily's hand. "Nice rings, Emily," she says. Only I think she means it. It must be a girl thing.

"Thanks," replies Emily. "The Sibling Silencer is, like, my favorite product of all time. Awesome idea!"

"Hi, Chris!" I call out as casually as if I had just seen one of my seventh-grade classmates at the mall. I'm starting to see how the whole celebrity thing could go to someone's head. Not mine, of course, but, you know, someone's.

The whole gang follows Chris into the building. It's no Sure Things, Inc. office, with our pizza topping machine and foosball table, that's for sure—but it's still pretty nice.

"Hey, Billy!" One of Chris Fernell's assistants yells. "Smile!"

I'm not the most photogenic person, but I'm caught so off guard that I look over anyway. Her camera **pops!** and out prints a photo of me.

"You need to sign it, Billy!" she says, placing a purple marker in my hand. "We're going to put you on the wall!"

I sign the photo, and underneath it I write *Sure Things, Inc.* Only that's when I realize I'm not Sure Things, Inc.—I'm Sure Things, Inc. with Manny. Manny is my partner and he's nowhere in the photo. He must feel bad. I never meant to take the spotlight from my best friend. I look over at him, but he's whispering away with Emily about something, which then makes *me* feel bad. What are they whispering about without me?

"Come, sit," Chris Fernell says, leading us into a meeting room. "Let's just go over the TV show rules one more time."

"It's a two-part special TV show contest where young inventors present their ideas and the judges choose which one will be made," I say quickly. Manny's face turns a little red. Oh no. This whole TV show was Manny's idea, and here I am blabbing away like it was mine!

"And the Hyenas will put the team logo on the winning product, with me as the spokes-man for the advertising," Carl adds.

"Love it!" chirps Chris. "So, how do we let kids know about the contest? Of course we'll promote it on my TV shows, but what else?"

"We could announce it on the Sure Things website," Emily suggests.

I can hear Manny adding the "Inc." to Emily's sentence in his head. He never just calls it "Sure Things." But both of us remain silent.

"Then KIDS FROM ALL OVER THE WORLD can know about it and enter," Emily continues. "After all, that's how we met Abby."

"Okay. Okay. But how are we going to get kids from across the world to this TV studio?" Chris says, rubbing his chin thoughtfully.

"That would be pretty expensive," Abby says. "And that would leave out lots of kids with good ideas who couldn't afford to come here. What if we have a live video chat so that any kid anywhere in the world could enter? You could set up big TV monitors on the stage so that the judges and the live studio audience and the viewers at home can all see kids from anywhere, and their ideas."

Boy, Abby is really smart. The more she talks, the more impressed I am.

"Fantastic!" booms Chris, slamming his palms onto the table. "I love it! Kids in the studio. Kids from around the world on video feed, all broadcast live! This is going to be huge! Big fun! Big ratings! Big ad dollars!"

We get up from the table. The meeting is adjourned.

"It was nice to meet you in person, Abby," I say. "If you'd like to stop by Sure Things, Inc. sometime, I'd be happy to show you around."

"Coolness," says Abby as she heads off to meet up with her mom.

A short while later as I climb into Dad's sensible hybrid sedan, I almost wish that I was just a regular kid again, instead of a partner in Sure Things, Inc. But not because I don't want to be an inventor. Because I would have loved to enter this very cool contest.

Chapter Five

Visitors

WE ARRIVE HOME PAST THE USUAL TIME WE EAT dinner, which means Dad won't have time to whip together one of his kitchen creations. My mouth starts to water at the thought of ordering in a pizza.

No such luck.

"I prepared dinner this morning," says Dad, pulling a casserole dish from the fridge. "A few seconds in the microwave and we'll be chowing down on MANGO-PARSNIP-HERRING SUPREME!"

Oh joy.

After a dinner filled with excited talk about the TV show and Dad's casserole, I head to my room where I read an e-mail from Mom.

Hi Honey,

I can't tell you how excited I am about your TV show. I'm also very pleased that Emily will be part of it and that you guys are getting along so well. How's it going with Carl? What's it like to work with one of your heroes?

I am so sorry about your birthday, honey. I'm not sure if I can video chat on that day, but I will definitely try. Which makes me realize I didn't even ask you—what are your plans for the big day?

Gotta run.

Love you lots,

Mom

I don't know what I want to do on my birthday. But the only thing I really want is for

Mom to be here. And she might not even be able to video chat.

I arrive at the office the next day just as Manny finishes placing a notice on the Sure Things, Inc. website asking for young inventors to take part in the TV special.

"We went live with this about five minutes ago," Manny says. "And we already have twenty-six kids who've signed up—including one from Bora Bora. This is going to be HUGE!"

Manny and I get busy nailing down an outline for how the TV special will go. We need to get this to Chris ASAP so he can sign off on it and get things moving.

"So I think Chris opens the show and gets everyone jazzed," Manny begins. He's talking and typing at the same time. I've seen him do this before, but it always amazes me. "He explains the premise, lets viewers know that our contestants come from all over the world, then introduces the five judges."

"Maybe we can alternate between a contestant

there in the studio and one from far away up on the monitor," I suggest.

"I like, I like," says Manny, his fingers typing away in high gear. I can't help but think he sounds like Chris Fernell.

"So how do you think we should wrap up the first day's show?" I ask.

Before Manny can reply, I hear a knock at the door. Manny and I look at each other. Very few people ever visit us here at the office.

I get up and open the front door. Abby is standing there, smiling.

"Hi, Billy. I thought I'd take you up on your offer to come visit," she says.

"Sure!" I say, maybe a bit too enthusiastically. "Come on in. Looks who's here, Manny."

Without missing a keystroke, Manny turns and says, "Hi, Abby. Welcome to the World Headquarters of Sure Things, Inc."

He just loves saying that.

"Let me show you around," I say. "This is my workbench." I point to the pile of stuff in my corner of the office.

"So this is where the magic happens, huh?" says Abby, her eyes opening wide as she looks over the parts scattered across my workbench. "Cool!"

"And this is where Manny works his magic," I say, leading Abby over to Manny's desk.

"I saw that the news of the TV show went live on your website a few minutes ago," she says.

"How did you know?" I ask.

Abby pulls out her smartphone. "I've set up my phone to send me alerts for any activity on the Sure Things, Inc. website."

It only takes Abby about three minutes to fit right in here. Doing this show with her is going to be fun.

"Whatcha working on now?" she asks Manny, looking over his shoulder.

"We're banging out a show outline for Chris."

Abby quickly reads through what Manny has written.

"One of us should probably explain the scoring system to the contestants," she suggests.

"Good idea," I say. "I can do that."

Briiiiiing!

Manny's phone rings. He keeps typing with one hand, while he swipes his phone's screen and answers the call on speakerphone.

"Sure Things, Inc., how can I help you?" he says.

"Hi, this is Kathy Jenkins. I'm a reporter for '**Right Next Door**,'" says a voice from the phone.

"Right Next Door" is a section of my town's website. In addition to articles, it also contains the local blog and community newsletters. Dad really likes those—he keeps submitting his recipes to be featured as a Yum Pick of the Month, but no luck yet. Shocking.

"I'd love to do a piece about Sure Things, Inc. and your upcoming TV special," Kathy continues.

Manny looks at me and shrugs.

"Why not?" I say.

"Sounds great, Kathy," says Manny. "When would you like to come by?"

"How's tomorrow?" asks Kathy.

"Okay. See you then."

More publicity for the TV show and the company. Nothing bad about that.

A few minutes later, there's another knock at the door. Philo, who was sleeping on his doggy bed before, looks up at me as if to say, "Someone else?" I rub my eyes and get the door.

At the door is a tall blond woman with her hair up in a bun. She looks very businesslike. She extends her hand.

"Kathy Jenkins," she says, shaking my hand *way* too firmly.

I guess "tomorrow" means today in the world of journalism!

"My daughter Samantha won't stop talking about what a GREAT INVENTOR you are," she says. "She is in your inventor's club. And she's your biggest fan!"

Oh yeah, Samantha. She's a sixth grader in the inventor's club who asked me to sign her Billy Sure T-shirt. She also who wrote me a poem, and she calls herself a "Billy Surette," and she gives me chocolate in the hallways on occasion.

"Of course," I reply. "Samantha is very . . . uh, enthusiastic."

"So, let's get right to the interview," says Kathy. She swipes a few things off my workbench and sits down. I'm a little annoyed, because she didn't even ask, but I don't say anything. Abby and Manny are quiet too. "Tell me how Sure Things, Inc. began."

"Well, it started with the All Ball," I begin. "I came up with idea, and Manny came up with the plan to get it out on shelves. That's Manny, my business partner."

"Hello," says Manny between keystrokes.

Kathy writes everything down in a notebook on her lap. But she isn't just writing my responses—she's jotting down notes about our office space. I can see one of her notes says PIZZA STAIN ON RUG. Hey, it's not my fault that Manny opted for a slice of triple-sauce pizza today.

"So after you started Sure Things—"

"Um, *we* started Sure Things, Inc.," I correct her. "Manny and I created the company together."

"So, at what age did you know that you would grow up to be a great inventor?" she asks, totally ignoring my comment about Manny.

"Um, well, I had my first invention idea in first grade," I say.

"And the inventor's club? How much do you love working with Samantha?"

"Uh, Samantha is great," I say. "Actually, the inventor's club was Manny's idea."

"So tell me about the upcoming TV show," Kathy snips.

"That was actually MANNY'S IDEA too," I explain. "We were going to look for new ideas from young inventors through our website, but Manny, as he usually does, kicked it up a level and suggested the TV show."

I really don't want Manny to be left out of this article.

"So I see on your website that you are one of the judges," Kathy says. "And so is Carl Bourette, the baseball player! How exciting."

"Yes, it's great to be working with Carl," I say. "There are actually five judges. Manny is one of them, and—"

"This is all great, Billy," Kathy interrupts. "Can I get a picture for the article?"

"Sure," I say, standing up. Unlike the photo at the TV studio, this time I ask, "Manny?" He stands and walks over next to me.

"Actually, since your name is in the company title, I'd like to just get you in the picture, Billy," says Kathy. "Sure Things and all."

Manny walks back to his desk. My heart sinks.

"Smile, Billy!" Kathy says. I force a smile

and she snaps the picture. "Thanks so much for your time. I can't wait to tell Samantha all about our little chat."

She jots down one more comment in her notebook—this time about Philo, who, according to her, LOOKS LIKE A DOG BUT SMELLS LIKE A SKUNK and hurries out the door.

"Manny, I am so sorry," I say.

"Not your fault," says Manny. "And you know me, I'm not about the fame."

Then he's back at work, banging away on his keyboard. Abby looks over his shoulder and doesn't say anything.

I know Manny says that it's okay, but I also know him too well. This is the first time since we started working together that I can feel

that he might be a little jealous. Which, of course, is the last thing I would ever want. My name may be in the company title, but without Manny, there is no Sure Things, Inc., and I'm just a kid fooling around with inventions in my garage.

He won't ever tell me, but I can see that Manny is unhappy.

And if Manny is unhappy, I'm unhappy.

Chapter Six

The Next Big Thing, Part One

IT'S SATURDAY. THE BIG DAY. THE FIRST DAY OF the two-part live TV event, which we all agreed to call—unsurprisingly—*Sure Things, Inc. and the Hyenas Present the Next Big Thing!*

I bound from bed extra early. Although the show will be broadcast live late this afternoon, we need to get to the TV studio early to get ready.

After a quick shower I get dressed and hurry downstairs. Even though I'm early, Emily is already at the kitchen table. Dad puts the finishing touches on a special breakfast of pancakes—not green-bean pancakes or artichoke pancakes or rutabaga pancakes—just pancakes—and shakes his head.

"Sorry about the PLAIN OLD BORING PANCAKES," says Dad as he places a steaming stack onto each of our plates. "Not enough time to make them extra special this morning."

I gobble them down. They are delicious. They are also the first food Dad has cooked in a long time that did not need the Gross-to-Good Powder.

"You're right at the top of 'Right Next Door,' you know, Mr. Celebrity," says Emily, who has gotten very skillful at using her knife and fork without creating a symphony of clanging rings. It takes her only a few tries to cut through the soft pancakes.

She shows me her phone, which is open to the website for "Right Next Door." Sure enough, my photo is at the top of the page.

I cringe at the headline: BILLY SURE—A SURE THING!

Then I focus in on the photo. It's just me

with that dumb-looking forced smile. My cringing goes into high gear. And then it gets worse.

Billy Sure, the twelve-year-old kid entrepreneur, is, on first glance, like any other seventh grader at Fillmore Middle. But on second glance, he is so much more.

Not only is Billy the successful inventor of his company, Sure Things, Inc., but he is adding "exceptionally awesome TV show star" to his name. Today Billy will be featured on his very own TV special, *Sure Things, Inc. and the Hyenas Present the Next Big Thing!*

"Billy is really amazing!" says Samantha Jenkins, a sixth grader at Fillmore Middle and Billy's very best friend. "We are all excited to watch him on TV!"

Samantha, who goes on to say that Billy is charming and handsome, also

wrote him a poem, published exclusively
by "Right Next Door:"

First it was the All Ball,
Now he's on a TV show,
Billy Sure is my doll,
And now you all know!

The article continues to talk about me. Not
once does it mention Manny. Never mind how
EMBARRASSING it is for me, I hope Manny
doesn't see this for his own sake. But of course,
there is practically no chance of that.

"You know what would be nice," Emily
says, popping the final bite of pancake into
her mouth. "If you got a business partner. Oh,
wait! I forgot. You already have one. I guess the
reporter who wrote this article also forgot."

As usual, Emily is a big help.

After breakfast Emily and I get into Dad's
car to head to the TV station. It's hard to believe
that in a few hours I'm going to be on TV, live
to millions of people all around the world.

We arrive at the station and meet up with Manny, whose parents drove him and will be sitting in the audience with Dad. A few moments later Abby and her mom arrive.

"Have a wonderful time, all of you," says Mrs. Nielson, giving Abby a big hug.

"Knock 'em dead!" booms Mr. Reyes. "Another home run for Sure Things, Inc.!"

"I'm really proud of both of you," says Dad, giving Emily and me high fives. "I'm planning a special celebratory dinner in your honor for tonight after the show!"

Lucky us.

As the grown-ups walk away, I realize again how much I miss Mom. If she were here now, she'd be sitting in the audience with Dad, feeling so proud of us. It's not just about her being here for my birthday. It's about missing her all the time. What is so important that she's doing for the government, anyway?

I'm shaken out of my gloomy thoughts by a voice so sharp it could cut through glass.

"Here are our judges!" shrieks Chris Fernell.

"Welcome to the big day. It's show time! You excited? You nervous?

"Come on, I'll bring you into the studio," he says. Manny, Emily, Abby, and I look at each other, shrug a collective shrug, and follow Chris.

We come to a large door labeled: STUDIO PERSONNEL ONLY! DO NOT ENTER! Chris pulls the door open and we all walk through. It only lasts for a moment, but for the first time since all this started, I feel like a big shot.

The TV studio is a beehive of activity. People push large TV cameras into position, talking into headsets. Others walk by carrying chairs, pitchers of water, or clipboards. Still others stand up on tall ladders hanging glittering stars in front of long curtains at the back of the set, while some stand on even taller ladders, adjusting lights to illuminate that set. The constant hum makes me think of an actual beehive.

The set itself features a small stage in the center. On one side of the set is a podium with

"Chris Fernell" spelled out in fancy letters. I think they flew that in from his studio in Los Angeles. On the other side is a long table with signs lined up at the front edge. Each judge has his or her name on one of the signs.

"Not so high!" shouts a woman with a headset and clipboard to a man hanging a star.

Chris leads us over to a woman standing at a tall desk. Three TV monitors line the desk. The woman is wearing a headset and is juggling three clipboards as people crowd around her, bombarding her with questions. Apparently, the more clipboards a person has, the more important he or she is.

I wonder if we'll get clipboards.

Chris scoots us around the outside of the crowd.

"Ann!" he shouts. Moving as one, the crowd steps back to let Chris—and all of us—in closer. "I'd like you to meet our judges: Billy,

Manny, Emily, and Abby," says Chris. "Guys, this is Ann Liveton, our director."

"Great to meet you all," says Ann, as three more clipboards are shoved in her face. She grabs each one, scans the papers attached to it, then quickly scribbles her initials and hands each clipboard back. "WHERE'S CARL?"

The entire studio suddenly breaks into applause. I turn around and spot Carl Bourette walking toward us.

"Nice shot yesterday, Carl!" shouts the man on the ladder. "An upper deck dinger!"

"Go, Hyenas!" yells a woman placing a water glass by each seat at the judges table.

Emily and Manny look confused. I smile. "Carl hit another game-winning homer in last night's Hyenas game," I explain.

"Hey, guys, sorry I'm late," says Carl. "Had to do a bunch of interviews."

We're lucky to get Carl during the preseason, and actually picked the dates for our show based on a rare time that the Hyenas had a couple of days off in a row. "It's okay," I say.

"The judges are in the house!" Chris shouts. "Let's go huddle over by your table."

The five of us gather at the table.

"So let's review the scoring rules," says Chris.

"Okay," I begin. "We've divided the judging into five categories—originality, functionality, usefulness, marketability, and ease of manufacturing. Each invention will be scored in each of these categories, rated on a scale from one to five. At the end of today's show, we'll total up the scores and pick the six highest scoring ideas. These six inventors will move on to the finals tomorrow."

"Works for me!" says Chris. "So, why don't you judges head to the green room. We've got SNACKS AND STUFF. I'll be in to join you in a little bit."

"Snacks and stuff" hardly begins to cover what is waiting for us backstage in the green room. Sandwiches of all kinds, five varieties of chips, salads, cakes, sodas, juice, on and on.

Oddly enough, even with all this incredible-looking food, I'm not hungry. Preshow nerves, maybe? Not sure.

"I can't eat anything either," says Abby, stepping up next to me. "I get this way before a big test or if I have to present a paper to my class. I'm okay in a small group, but I get pretty nervous in front of an audience."

"Yeah, me too," I say.

"You must be excited, not only getting to be on TV but also getting to pick your next big invention," says Carl, stepping up next to Abby and me at the food table and stuffing an entire peanut butter sandwich into his mouth.

Clearly, he has no preshow nerves. I guess when you play baseball in front of thirty thousand people every day, doing a TV show is no big deal.

"Yeah, I'm excited and a little nervous," I admit.

"No worries, Billy, you'll do great! I remember my rookie year, my first game. I was so nervous that I put on my teammate's SHOES.

They were TWO SIZES TOO BIG! I flopped around the field for the first two innings! Man, my teammates never let me forget that!"

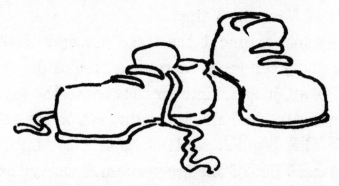

As Carl talks, I notice that across the room, Manny has pulled Emily aside and is leaning in, speaking quietly into her ear. He looks very serious, even for Manny. Emily has a shocked expression on her face like she is totally surprised by what Manny is telling her.

This is now the second time I've seen Manny and Emily whispering about something. What are they talking about?

Maybe Manny is even more upset than I thought about being left out of the photo and "Right Next Door" article. Maybe he's telling Emily that he doesn't want to work with me anymore. Maybe he doesn't even want to be my friend. All this just as we are about to tell the whole world that we're looking for Sure Things' Next Big Thing!

At that moment the stage manager walks into the green room carrying a clipboard.

"Okay, judges, time for the show," she says, pointing to the hallway leading out to the set.

THIS IS IT. No time to talk to Manny. As I head out of the green room, I worry that this show might be the last thing we ever do together.

I step onto the set and hear the buzz of the audience. The place is packed. I squint through the bright lights and spot Dad, Mr. and Dr. Reyes, and Mrs. Nielson right in the front row. Dad is waving wildly at me. I wave back.

I take my seat at the long judges' table. A stack of printed forms sits in front of me. Each form has a place for the contestant's name, invention, and a list of the five scoring categories for me to fill in. Emily sits on one side of me and Abby on the other. Manny and

Carl are each at one end of the table. I realize then that I am front and center—and Manny is off to the side—once again.

Across the set, Chris Fernell stands at his podium. He fiddles with his microphone as a makeup person dabs some powder onto his cheeks and a hair stylist sprays some stuff onto his head.

The stage manager steps out.

"We will be live on the air in ONE MIN-UTE!" she announces to the audience. "Is everyone ready for some big-time cheering?"

"Yeah!" comes the loud reply from the audience.

"Oh, we can do better than that, can't we?"

"YEAH!" comes the thunderous response.

"All right! Thirty seconds!" the stage manager shouts.

I feel my heart start to pound. I begin to wonder if this whole thing is a really bad idea.

"Twenty seconds!"

I look over at the other judges. Emily looks cool and collected. Abby is chewing on her lower lip. Manny is casually checking his phone. Carl smiles and flashes me a thumbs up. I'm suddenly really glad we asked him to be here.

"Ten seconds!"

Here we go.

"And five . . . four . . . three . . . two . . . one! Showtime! We are on the air!"

Chapter Seven

Showtime!

MUSIC BLARES AND SPOTLIGHTS SWEEP THE ROOM, lighting up the glittering stars on the set.

"Hi, everyone, and welcome to a very special live television event!" says Chris.

A thunderous cheer explodes from the audience.

"Sure Things, Inc. and the Hyenas Present the Next Big Thing, Part One!" Chris continues. The name of the show is definitely a mouthful, but the Hyenas' management insisted on it.

But it doesn't seem to matter to the studio audience, because they give another big cheer.

"You all know about Sure Things, Inc., the company that brought you the All Ball, the Sibling Silencer, the Gross-to-Good Powder, and more."

I glance at Abby, who has a huge grin on her face. Maybe I've just gotten used to people making a big deal about my inventions. I kinda forget how AMAZING it feels. But Abby just heard the name of her invention announced on a TV show airing all over the world—and that's pretty cool.

"Ever wonder how the folks at Sure Things, Inc. get their great ideas for new inventions? For new products that make your lives easier and more fun? For the Next Big Thing?"

Chris is on a roll.

"Well, today and tomorrow, you'll find out! Young inventors from around the world will present their ideas to our panel of judges. At the end of today's show, the judges will narrow the contestants down to six finalists who will return tomorrow when our judges will pick one winner, one invention to be Sure Things'

Next Big Thing! Now let's meet our judges!"

A camera swings around to face the judges' table. Then the camera rolls closer and closer, coming right at me!

"Judge number one is the guy who gives Sure Things, Inc. its name. He's the kid inventor who has taken the world by storm. He's the heart and soul of Sure Things, Inc., a seventh-grader, and the president of the Fillmore Middle School Inventors Club. GIVE IT UP FOR BILLY SURE!"

The audience applauds loudly. Several "whoops" and "wows" cut through the clapping. I see Dad standing in the front row, clapping his hands over his head. Then I remember that I'm on TV, and that the camera is zoomed in on a close-up of my face. I wave weakly and force a smile.

"Judge number two is Billy's partner in all things Sure Things. He's the kid with the computer brain, the Mozart of marketing, the Beethoven of business, the Vivaldi of variables. Put your hands together for the chief financial officer of Sure Things, Inc., Manny Reyes!"

Ever the cool customer, Manny gives a small wave to the camera.

"Judge number three is also part of the Sure Things, Inc. family—quite literally, in fact. She's a freshman at Fillmore High School, a straight-A science student, the originator of the Gross-to-Good Powder, and oh yeah, she's Billy's big sister. Give a great big welcome to Emily Sure!"

Emily smiles and waves at the camera, then at the audience with both hands. She's absolutely loving being in the spotlight. Her ten rings catch the bright lights, reflecting colored lights in all directions.

"Judge number four was once in the same boat as the contestants on today's program. She entered the previous Next Big Thing competition and won! She's a math whiz, writes computer code faster than you can whip up a shopping list, and is the inventor of the Sibling Silencer. Let's hear it for Abby Nielson!"

Abby smiles and waves at the crowd like she's been doing this her whole life. Which makes me smile—FOR REAL.

"And finally, judge number five. He needs no introduction—but I'll introduce him anyway."

Now it's Chris's turn to crank his fake TV smile up to its brightest setting.

"You know him as a guest on my show. You also know him as the all-star shortstop for the Hyenas, the slick-fielding, hard-hitting Carl Bourette!"

Again the crowd bursts into cheers and applause.

"What you may not know, though, is that Carl and the Hyenas have agreed to endorse the winning invention. Carl will be the spokesman for the product, which will also have the Hyenas' team logo on it. Way to go, Carl. You've just scored another home run in my book!"

A swell of dramatic music blares from the studio's speakers.

"And now," Chris begins in a super-serious voice. "The time has come to meet our first contestant. Here to show us his invention idea is Asher!"

A tall boy with curly blond hair walks out and steps onto the stage. He is carrying a paper bag in one hand and holding his other hand behind his back.

"Hi!" he begins, sounding very nervous. "Um, I am Asher."

He sets his bag down on the floor, then pulls his hand out from behind his back. He's holding a long wooden stick with a small wooden hand attached to the end.

"This is a regular, everyday backscratcher," Asher explains. He then proceeds to reach behind his head with the stick and use the hand part to scratch way down in the middle of his back.

"Backscratchers are great, but what if you need something for other hard-to-reach places?"

ewwww!

Asher reaches into his bag and pulls out a short plastic stick with what looks like a finger on the end.

"This is my first invention, the AUTOMATIC NOSE PICKER," Asher says. He sticks the plastic finger into his nose and presses a button, then pulls the finger out.

I don't even want to describe what's sitting on the end of the finger.

"My second invention is the AUTOMATIC EAR CLEANER," Asher says, putting the nose picker down and reaching into his bag.

Out comes a short metal handle with a cotton swab on the end.

"It works like this." Asher sticks the padded end up to his ear and flips a switch. The pad spins around and around, and then he pulls it out. Words can't describe what Asher pulls out of his ear. Not only is it gross, the automatic ear cleaner is totally unsafe.

Asher finishes his pitch. "If my invention is *picked*, I would like Sure Things, Inc. to help me pull all this together into a combo backscratcher, nose picker, and ear cleaner. Thank you."

I hear a lot of groans, a few claps, and perhaps even some gagging as Asher puts the various pieces of his invention—and his body—back into his bag and walks off the stage.

I jot down my scores in each of the categories, 5 being the best—originality 2, functionality 3, usefulness 1, marketability 1, ease of manufacturing 5.

"Thank you, Asher," says Chris. "That was quite . . . unusual. Our next contestant joins us all the way from Italy. For you folks at home, she'll be right there on your TV screen. For our studio audience and judges, please turn your attention to the back of the stage."

A huge TV monitor, as big as a movie theater screen, drops down. The other four judges and I swivel our chairs around.

"Ladies and gentleman, please welcome Maria!"

The giant screen comes to life. And there stands a girl with shiny black hair.

"Hello, everybody around the world," she begins. "I am Maria. I live in Italy, and I have an idea for a great invention."

Maria stands beside a table with a small wooden box with tiny holes in it, a fly swatter, a spray can, and a big loose-leaf binder.

"Everyone knows that flying bugs are TERRIBLE PESTS," Maria continues. "They bite you, they get in your food at picnics, and they are very annoying. But at the same time, some of us like to collect bugs."

Maria grabs the loose-leaf binder and opens it. There, attached to the pages, are bugs—everything from beautiful butterflies to really gross giant mosquitoes.

"I enjoy collecting and studying bugs, but catching them can be hard."

She picks up the fly swatter and then opens the wooden box. A bug flies out.

"Of course you can use a fly swatter."

THWaPPP!

Maria swats the bug against the table, squashing it into a gooey mess.

"But that leaves the bug all squished and no good for your collection."

My curiosity is piqued. I can't wait to see where this is going.

"My invention is a nontoxic bug spray that freezes bugs in midair in perfect condition. That way you can simply take them out of the air and place them right into your collection book."

Maria picks up the spray can. She releases another bug from the box, then sprays it. When the spray clears, the bug is floating in midair. Then the bug shatters into tiny pieces and crumbles to the floor.

"I would like help from Sure Things, Inc. to

perfect the spray so it can help bug collectors all over the world. Thank you."

The big screen goes dark and the audience applauds.

Emily leans over to me. "That's the GROSSEST THING I ever saw," she whispers.

"What about the booger and earwax kid?" Abby asks, leaning in from my other side.

Emily just shudders in response.

Hmm . . . this is a tougher one to score. As I ponder my scoring, Chris moves right on to the next contestant.

"Our next contestant is a student at Graham Middle School," Chris begins.

Graham Middle School is in the town next to mine. There's an intense rivalry between their teams and Fillmore's.

"And he's a big fan of KUNG FU MOVIES. Please welcome Terry!"

A short boy walks out onto the stage. He is dressed in a martial arts outfit complete with a beginner's yellow belt. I notice bright orange sweatbands on his wrists and ankles. He brings his palms together at his chest and bows to the audience.

"Thank you. My name is Terry and I love all kinds of martial arts movies. Even though I have studied karate and kung fu, I still can't come close to doing the stuff I see in the movies. That's why I invented KUNG FU SWEATBANDS. With these on my wrists and ankles I can do all kinds of awesome moves, just like my favorite action stars. I have had a little trouble controlling the sweatbands, and that's why I'd like help from Sure Things, Inc. I'll demonstrate."

Terry squeezes his left wristband. All four orange sweatbands start to glow. Then he

begins a routine. He throws kicks and punches with amazing speed. He leaps into the air, spins three times, then lands in a split and pops back up to his feet.

But that's when the sweatbands go berserk. Terry starts punching and kicking at amazing speed. His body is bucking everywhere. He CAN'T STOP!

"Help! I can't shut these off!" Terry cries, desperately trying to grab his left wristband with his right hand.

Members of the TV crew come rushing out onto the stage. As they reach for Terry's arms and legs, one gets karate chopped in the arm. Another gets kicked in the shoulder. *Ouch!*

The out-of-control sweatbands launch Terry into the air, feet first, heading right toward a TV camera. He lands a kick right on the camera's lens, breaking it.

Terry finally manages to grab his left wrist and switches off the bands. He lands on his feet and bows to the audience again.

"Like I said, these need work. Thank you."

Then, sweating and breathing heavily, Terry leaves the stage.

This is a hard one to score. And it certainly would need *a lot* of work to get it ready for the marketplace. Not to mention trial runs I'm pretty sure I don't want to be anywhere near. As I mark up my score sheet, a new TV camera is hooked up, ready to go. That's the speed of showbiz!

The show rolls along smoothly from this point on. A series of inventions are presented, including some fantastic ideas that I'm certain will make it to the finals, and a few that are a clear-cut no. For example, one girl presents an app that lets you reserve your table in the school cafeteria. No way would the lunch staff

accept this one—at least not in my school.

Then there is a hat that makes your hair grow faster when you wear it. This one I don't get at all. Why would people want to grow hair faster? That would just mean more trips to see the hairdresser. Oh, and the hair it grows comes out smelling like pickles. Again, the appeal is lost on me, but I see Emily nod enthusiastically. "Nothing a little perfume can't fix," I hear her say under her breath.

And finally, probably the most frequently proposed idea ever—the TIME MACHINE. Many people have suggested it. Some have even come up with rough designs. But I'm telling you, it's impossible. Unless, of course, someone invents it way in the future and uses it to come back to our time to show us how to build one.

When the final contestant is finished, the five judges huddle together, comparing scores.

"Well, the tension is so thick you could cut it with a knife," says Chris. "The judges are deciding which six inventors get to come back and show off their ideas again tomorrow night, when only one will be chosen as—THE NEXT BIG THING!"

For this first round, there's no time for discussion. We're simply adding up the scores. When we're ready, Carl stands up and announces the six finalists. All of my favorites made it in! We'll get a closer look at their ideas tomorrow.

"That's it for tonight, but don't you dare do anything else tomorrow, because we'll be back for the finals of *Sure Things, Inc. and the Hyenas Present the Next Big Thing!*"

And then the show is over.

Chris walks over to the judges table and shakes each of our hands. "Fantastic, guys, just great," he says. "And the best is yet to come. See you tomorrow!"

A few minutes later we are all backstage in the green room. Dad, Mrs. Nielson, and Manny's parents join us.

"You guys were great!" says Dad, giving Emily and me big hugs.

"We really didn't do anything," Emily points out. "We just wrote down our scores."

"You looked very handsome on TV," Dr. Reyes says to Manny, who smiles that forced smile of his.

"I enjoyed all of it," Mrs. Nielson says. "You looked so grown-up, Abby."

"Thanks, Mom."

"You guys were all real pros out there," says Carl. "Like you've been on TV a whole bunch of times. Nice job, kids. I'll see you all tomorrow."

"See ya, Carl," I say. That's my friend, Carl Bourette. Unbelievable.

On the car ride home I think about tomorrow's show and how it will affect my future. After all, this isn't just a fun TV show. This is how we're picking the next invention for Sure Things, Inc. Meanwhile, Emily's eyes are glued to her phone, her rings clacking away on the screen as she texts probably the whole world about her day in the spotlight.

Chapter Eight

Between Two acts

I ARRIVE HOME STILL BUZZING WITH EXCITEMENT. But I know I have to go to bed quickly. It'll be another big day tomorrow. I'm brushing my teeth, staring out the bathroom window, when I see a car pull up. Huh. That's weird. A woman exits the car and steps up to the door. I can't make out who it is from this far away.

This is strange. We haven't had many people over since Mom started traveling—Dad leaves his paintbrushes around sometimes, and I think he is a little embarrassed to have company come and see how forgetful he is.

Ring aaaaaa diiiiing!!!

Our doorbell rings.

"I'll get it!" I yell.

I walk over to the door and peep through the hole, curious about who is outside. If I don't recognize the woman, I won't let her in the house, and I'll call Dad for help. But when I look through, I'm stunned to realize I *do* recognize the woman. It's KATHY JENKINS from "Right Next Door!" I wish she really was next door—or at any other door—at this particular moment.

I open the door just to tell her to come back another time, but she waltzes in anyway.

"Billy Sure, kid of the hour!" she screeches, her notebook at the ready. "I know this is a little unexpected, but the 'Right Next Door' readers just loved the last article. I know Samantha was really proud."

I can feel my face get red. If I wasn't so worried about everything else, I'd be pretty embarrassed about her poem.

"I just wanted to ask you a few questions," Kathy says. "Just two, I promise."

"Um, okay," I say.

"What do you think of the finalists for *The Next Big Thing*?" she asks, pen at the ready.

"I think they're great," I say. "Really creative. I'm sure Manny will be able to market them . . ."

"Yes, yes, Manny," Kathy says, almost like she's annoyed. "And next, who do you think will win the competition?"

I have a feeling about one of the inventions, but I don't say anything.

"It's up in the air. I'd have to ask the other judges what they think," I say. Kathy takes note of it, but I look into her notebook and see she's misquoted me. She wrote I'LL HAVE TO ASK SAMANTHA WHAT SHE THINKS. Which is totally not what I said!

"Thanks for your time, Billy," Kathy says. "Look for yourself in 'Right Next Door' tomorrow."

And just like that, Kathy leaves.

I have trouble sleeping that night.

When I finally doze off, I spend the night

dreaming about kung fu kicks, frozen bugs, and indescribably gross earwax.

After I wake up, I get dressed and hurry down for breakfast. Emily is already at the table. Dad is whipping up a celebratory omelet filled with artichoke, pickled tuna, raisins, and a few things that I can't identify.

"Ready for the big finale, guys?" he asks, placing a steaming omelet down in front of me. Emily passes me the salt shaker without even looking up from her phone.

"Yesterday was really fun," Emily says. "Though I was kinda disappointed that you and Manny didn't go for the time machine idea."

"Yeah, well, whoever comes up with a way to really make that one work . . . wow."

We eat in silence for a few minutes. Then I bring up what's been ON MY MIND since yesterday. "So, Emily, what were you and Manny talking about yesterday in the green room before the show?"

Emily flinches and looks a bit shocked. She

obviously didn't realize that I had seen her conversation with Manny.

"Nothing," she replied. "You know, um . . . the show and stuff."

Emily is a terrible liar.

"He wasn't talking about me, was he?" I ask.

"You know, not everything is about you, Billy," she snaps at me, quicker this time.

End of conversation. Still, something is most definitely up.

After breakfast I head to my room. I can't stop think thinking about Manny. I need to clear the air with him before we meet up for today's show. After all, we have to make a decision together that will affect the future of our company. And it's almost my birthday. I can't have him mad at me at a time like this. Or ever, actually.

I do something I rarely do. I pick up the phone and call Manny's cell. Normally when I want to get in touch with him I shoot off a text or an e-mail, but this is too important. I need to hear his voice and talk this out.

I dial, but the call goes right to Manny's voice mail. I send him a text . . . nothing back. Then an e-mail. Again, no reply.

This is **VERY STRANGE**. Manny always takes his calls, even when he's on another call. And he replies to his e-mails and texts instantly. In fact, we have a running joke that Manny usually replies to my texts even before I have finished composing them. Something is up. I have a bad feeling about this. Could he really be avoiding me?

The drive to the TV station this time is very quiet. Emily barely makes eye contact. I sit and worry about Manny. That's when I come up with an idea. What if I get Manny featured in one of his business journals! I do something very Manny-like and write a few e-mails on my phone while texting with a few other people.

We arrive at the TV station. As I get out of Dad's car, I see Manny talking to Abby. But as soon as they spot me, they both stop talking. They look uncomfortable, like they were just caught doing something they shouldn't be doing.

I want to know what's going on, but I can't ask Manny now, just as we are about to do something as important as this show. No, the Manny solution will have to wait. I try to shake off these worries and focus on the task at hand. Then I head into the station for part two!

Chapter Nine

The Next Big Thing, Part Two

THE SNACK SPREAD IN THE GREEN ROOM IS EVEN more impressive on the second day. Pizza with a bunch of toppings, giant subs with meats, cheeses, veggies, salads, and twelve kinds of cookies!

"Big day, partner," Manny says, taking a **GINORMOUS CHOMP** out of a slice of pizza. I can't help but think that Manny might have figured out how to unhinge his jaw. Kind of like a snake. But hey, at least he's talking to me, so I don't say anything. "The finalists are all good. It'll be fun to see them again going head to head."

"The scores were pretty close," Abby points out as she digs into a big bowl of salad. "I think I know which one I like best, but I'm going to keep an open mind when I see the finalists again."

Yesterday Abby was too nervous to eat anything. I guess she's not so nervous today.

"It's pretty cool to help choose the Next Big Thing," says Emily, slipping a cookie into her pocket for later. "As you know, Abby."

Abby smiles. Emily seems to like her a lot too.

"Hey, team, ready for action?" says Carl as he enters the green room and snatches two slices of pizza. "Time to pick us a winner."

Chris Fernell walks into the room. "Here they are. My judges!" he chirps, throwing his arms open wide. I used to wonder if people I saw on TV were any different in real life. I don't know about everyone, but Chris is . . . well, just Chris.

"Ready for the big day?" he says.

"Let's go do this," says Carl. Then he turns

and charges toward the studio as if he were leaving the locker room to go take his position at shortstop.

We find our seats at the judges table. Chris shuffles through some papers at his podium. I look out into the audience, and there is Dad in his same seat in the front row, waving.

The stage manager steps out onto the stage.

And . . . here we go again.

"Thirty seconds!" the stage manager shouts.

And even though I just did this yesterday, my heart starts to pound again.

"Ten seconds!"

This is it. I have the same feeling in my stomach that I always get just before a plane I'm on takes off.

"And five . . . four . . . three . . . two . . . one! We are on the air!"

The opening music fills the studio and the spotlights crisscross the stage.

"Hi, everyone, and welcome to part two of *Sure Things, Inc. and the Hyenas Present the Next Big Thing!*" Chris continues.

A big cheer explodes from the audience.

"On today's program we will be picking the winner, the young inventor whose idea will become Sure Things' Next Big Thing! And now, let's reintroduce our judges."

Chris runs through the introductions for each of us—word for word what he said yesterday. I think that's just in case someone missed part one. Then it's on to the first finalist.

"You might say finalist number one is a *shoe* in. She's eleven years old, and she's joined by her younger brother and sister. Let's give a big *NEXT BIG THING* welcome to Mallory!"

Mallory, who is tall with blond hair, steps up to the microphone. She is carrying a cloth bag.

"Hi, my name is Mallory. Thank you so much for having me back today. Yesterday I introduced my idea, and today I am here with my older brother, Jack, who's fifteen, and my little sister, Helen, who's six. You may be wondering why I brought them with me. Let me explain."

Mallory opens her cloth bag and pulls out what looks like an ordinary pair of shoes. They are brown and white and appear to be way too small for someone her age.

"Yesterday I presented my GROW-WITH-YOU SHOES," Mallory says. "What if you could buy one pair of shoes that actually grows along with you? Parents would save lots of money. And no more boring trips to the shoe store."

She walks over to her younger sister. "This prototype for the Grow-With-You Shoes is just the right size for Helen."

She hands the shoes to Helen.

"Go ahead and put them on."

Helen takes off the shoes she is wearing and slips the Grow-With-You Shoes onto her feet.

"How do those fit?" Mallory asks.

"They feel great!" Helen replies very enthusiastically. This is obviously rehearsed, but she's so cute that I can't help cracking up.

"Wonderful," says Mallory. "Okay, now take them off and hand them to Jack."

Helen pulls off the shoes and gives them to Jack, who is barefoot.

"Oh no!" says Jack, in an overly dramatic voice. "These shoes fit Helen. How could they possibly fit me, a fifteen-year-old with size 12 feet?"

Again, I smile. More than any of the contestants so far, Mallory has worked just as hard on her presentation as she did on her invention.

"Just try them on, Jack," says Mallory.

Jack slips his toes into the tiny shoes Helen has just handed him. Amazingly, the shoes GROW and STRETCH until they are the perfect size for Jack's feet!

It's nice to see the finalists for a second

time. I sneak a peek at the other judges' faces. Carl's mouth hangs open and his eyes are wide.

"The Grow-With-You Shoes," says Mallory. "Ready to grow, ready to go, ready to be Sure Things' Next Big Thing. Thank you."

The audience applauds as Mallory and her siblings walk off stage.

I have to say, I give this product very high scores.

"Thank you, Mallory," says Chris. "Our next contestant comes from right around the corner. In fact, he's a student at Fillmore Middle School, just like Billy Sure. Please welcome Ralph!"

When the All Ball first came out, everyone was pitching me ideas for new inventions. Things got so crazy that we came up with the idea for the Next Big Thing contest. I remember Ralph's idea for a POP-UP CHANGING TENT. He's been working hard on this idea ever since. I wasn't overly impressed when I saw him on the show yesterday, but I was outvoted by the other judges, so here he is in the finals. He has a backpack slung over one shoulder.

"My invention is the Pop-Up Changing Tent," says Ralph. "Picture this. You were in school all day. You played outside at recess. Your clothes got dirty. Your parents are picking you up to go to a special dinner at your grandmother's house. You're supposed to be clean and wearing clean clothes. But there's nowhere to change! What will you do? With my Pop-Up Changing Tent, you can change anywhere and have all the PRIVACY you could want."

Ralph slips off the backpack and pulls out a square piece of plastic. He presses a button in the center of the square and the plastic starts to expand. It pops open and continues to grow. In a few seconds a small tent stands beside Ralph.

"I bring my change of clothes," Ralph continues, pulling a button-down shirt and a clean pair of pants from his backpack, "slip into the Pop-Up Changing Tent . . ."

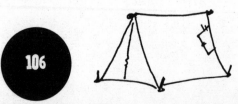

Ralph steps inside the tent. It shakes for few minutes, then suddenly collapses all around him, like shrink wrap.

Ralph's head pops out of a small opening. "Um, it still needs some work," he says. "That's why I think my tent should be the Next Big Thing. Thank you."

He manages to get his feet free and shuffles off the stage like a walking blue plastic bag.

Once again, Ralph does not get high marks from me. He's come up with a catchy name, but I just don't see it being all that useful. Especially because he could probably have just changed into clean clothes in the bathroom.

"Thanks, Ralph, and good luck getting out of that thing," says Chris as soon as Ralph leaves the stage. "Okay, judges and our studio audience, time to turn your attention to the big screen at the back of the stage."

The huge TV monitor drops from above.

"You folks at home keep your eyes glued to your TV screens as we welcome, all the way

from Ghana in West Africa, Afia!"

A young girl appears on the giant screen. She sits on the edge of a bed wearing a large metal helmet on her head. Wires lead from the helmet to a computer sitting on the night stand next to her bed. It kinda looks like a more sophisticated BEST TEST.

"Nice to see everyone again," she begins. "My invention is the DREAM MACHINE. You know how sometimes you have an amazing dream, but when you wake up you can't remember it? My Dream Machine takes all of your dreams and converts them into videos, which are then sent right to your e-mail address. In the morning you can watch your dream again and again."

Now *this* I like. Apparently the studio audience likes it too, as a buzz of conversation spreads through the studio.

Afia clicks on her computer screen. A video comes on showing her flying through the sky, looking down on the African countryside.

"This is a dream I had last week. I often dream that I can fly."

A group gasp comes from the studio audience. The video ends.

"There are, however, two problems right now with my Dream Machine that I have not been able to solve," Afia continues. "That is why I would like the help of Sure Things, Inc."

Afia swings her legs up and lies down on her bed. The huge helmet squishes her pillow.

"The first problem is that the helmet is uncomfortable. It makes it very hard to fall asleep," Afia explains. "So I need help making the helmet smaller and more comfortable."

I'm sure I could help her with that.

"The second problem is that everyone you dream about receives a copy of the video e-mailed right to them. As you can imagine, that can be very embarrassing. For example, if you dream about kissing your crush, that person would get a copy of the dream. If you dream about coming to school in just your underwear, your teacher would know about it when you show up the next day. This needs to be fixed."

I shudder to think about this happening. It's kind of like what happened with the CAT-DOG TRANSLATOR. Our inventions should never reveal our secrets. Still, there's something to Afia's Dream Machine.

"Thank you very much for this opportunity," says Afia. Then the screen goes dark.

"Wow!" says Chris. "I would hate for people to know my dreams! Why just the other night, I—well, never mind!"

The audience laughs. I think about some of the CRAZY DREAMS I've had and cringe at the thought that anyone else would actually be able to see them.

"Next up is Alexander," Chris says. "He's invented something that I believe we would have all found useful at one time or another. Alexander!"

A short boy with stubby legs strolls out onto the stage carrying a roll of toilet paper on a stick.

There is something very strange-looking about this boy. And also something kind of familiar. I thought the same thing when he presented his idea yesterday, but I just can't put my finger on who he reminds me of.

"Hello," he says. "I'm eleven years old and this is my invention."

His voice is surprisingly deep for an eleven-year-old kid. And why does it look like he needs to shave?

"My invention is a roll of toilet paper that never runs out," Alexander explains. "Have you ever been caught in the situation where you run out of toilet paper and

there is no extra roll around? Of course you have. Well, that will never happen again if Sure Things, Inc. helps me bring the NEVER-ENDING ROLL to the marketplace."

Alexander spins the toilet paper roll. The paper just keeps streaming off the roll, piling up on the stage. Amazingly, the roll doesn't seem to be getting any smaller!

Just as I'm beginning to think that this could be a contender for the big prize, Alexander starts to grow. Yes, I said GROW. He gets taller, and his face widens, and wrinkles form. Panic fills his eyes.

And that's when I finally recognize him.

"That's not really a kid!" I shout, standing up and pointing. "That's ALISTAIR SWIPED!"

Chapter Ten

Trouble in a Bubble

ALISTAIR SWIPED BACKS AWAY SLOWLY.

Swiped is an inventor who is best known for stealing other people's ideas—especially *our* ideas. He tried impersonating my mom to steal them, and he stole the first prototype for our Cat-Dog Translator. And he's done lots of other crooked stuff. He wouldn't know an original idea if it landed on his head.

"My Never-Ending Roll is still a good idea!" Swiped shouts. "Even though my MAKE-YOURSELF-YOUNG-AGAIN

POTION obviously needs some work, promotion from you could help my company, Swiped Stuff, Inc., get back in business!"

As he creeps away, Swiped trips over the pile of toilet paper on the floor. He falls on the ground and gets caught up in the paper. When he stands up again, he looks like a mummy. There's even toilet paper covering his eyes and mouth. (I'm no fan of Swiped, but for his sake I'm thankful the toilet paper is unused.) Two security guards grab him by the arms and escort him offstage. Soon the only thing left of Swiped is a pile of toilet paper.

"Well, that was unexpected!" says Chris, not

missing a beat. "I'd have to say that contestant is disqualified!"

The audience applauds.

I can't believe Swiped would try to fool Sure Things, Inc. into putting out his product. Actually, I guess I can believe it. I just can't believe that he thought he'd get away with it by pretending to be a kid.

"Let's go back to the giant video monitor for our next contestant," Chris says, moving things right along.

The huge screen drops down again. On the screen, a boy sits in a wheelchair in front of a large machine.

"Joining us from Japan is Hiroki. And I think if there's one word to describe his invention, it's FUN!"

"Hello. My name is Hiroki. I am happy to share my invention with you," he begins.

This invention impressed me when I saw it yesterday, and I'm sure I could help Hiroki work out the bugs. The machine he sits in front of has a monitor and keyboard, a joystick, a scanner, and a printer all built right in.

"I call my invention the HOMEWORK FUNNERIZER," Hiroki continues. "Simply put, it converts any homework assignment into a video game. Let me demonstrate."

Hiroki picks up several sheets of paper.

"This is my math homework. I must solve a series of equations involving fractions."

He puts the math assignment into the scanner. It flashes for a few seconds, then he takes the paper out.

"And this is my language homework. I am studying Mandarin Chinese."

Again, he scans the homework sheet.

"And finally, this is my history homework. I am learning about the great emperors in Japanese history."

Hiroki scans his history homework.

"Now I press a button, and the Homework Funnerizer creates a video game. I must win the video game by doing my homework assignments. If I do, the Funnerizer will convert the results back into homework answers which I can hand in to my teacher. Watch!"

Hiroki positions his wheelchair in front of the screen. He presses the start button. A fantasy world appears on the monitor filled with bubbling lava swamps, sprawling evergreen forests, and stone castles rising high into the sky.

Hiroki's on-screen avatar, a young warrior, clutches his sword tightly. Suddenly, a horde of monstrous creatures comes pouring out of the forest, rushing right at Hiroki! But there is something strange about the creatures.

One is half Cyclops, half troll. Another is two-thirds gnome, one-third giant. To defeat

cyclops half

troll half

the creatures Hiroki has to match the fractional parts to form whole monsters.

Once he completes this task, Hiroki stands at the gates to the castle. An ancient yellowed scroll appears filled with Japanese writing. Hiroki has to translate the scroll into Mandarin Chinese in order to open the gates.

When he finishes translating, the gates swing open. Inside the castle, Hiroki comes to a series of doors. On each door the name of a Japanese emperor is written. Hiroki has to go through the doors in the correct order—based on the order in which the emperors ruled—in order to reach and defeat the goblin king.

Hiroki finishes all the tasks. And just like that, the Homework Funnerizer converts the game back to completed homework assignments! **WOW!** As I'm imagining how much easier my English assignments would be as a video game, the printer starts printing out the assignments but ends up shredding the paper into confetti instead.

"This is the part I need help with," says Hiroki. "What good is a Homework Funnerizer if it is also a HOMEWORK SHREDDERIZER? If I win, I hope that Sure Things, Inc. can help me fix this. Thank you very much."

"Okay, gang," says Chris. "The time has come to meet our final finalist. He's thirteen and says he's been inventing things ever since he was six years old. Let's hear it for Greg!"

Out walks a boy wearing glasses. He has dark close-cropped hair. He holds a small box in his hand. There is a button on the top of the box.

"Hi, I'm Greg, and my invention is the NO-TROUBLE BUBBLE," he begins. "It protects you from just about anything—spitballs, darts, balls of any kind. You are always safe inside the No-Trouble Bubble."

This invention would be great, if it works. It reminds me of the PERSONAL FORCE FIELD BELT that Manny and I have been working on.

"I'd like to demonstrate the No-Trouble

Bubble for the judges, but I need a volunteer to go inside the bubble."

Greg looks right at me.

"I can't think of anyone better to test the No-Trouble Bubble than the great inventor himself, Billy Sure!"

The loudest cheer of the day goes up from the studio audience.

"How about it, Billy?" asks Chris.

I shake my head and try to smile politely. As I've said before, I am not a big fan of being in the spotlight.

The crowd roars even louder.

"Come on, Billy, how about it?" urges Chris.

"Don't you all want to see Billy in the bubble?" asks Greg, talking directly to the audience.

Cries of: "Yeah!" "Come on, Billy!" "Do it for us, Billy!" come from the crowd.

I shoot Manny a glance. He raises his eyebrows and tilts his head as if to say, "Give the people what they want."

Great. Thanks, Manny. Emily is no help

either. She waves her hand toward the stage, urging me to get up. Why couldn't Greg have chosen Emily instead?

I guess I don't have a choice. I stand up and walk to the stage as the crowd cheers wildly.

"It's such an honor to meet you, Billy," says Greg, shaking my hand.

"Nice to meet you too, Greg," I say. "So how does your invention work?"

Greg gives me the box. "Just press the button."

As soon as I press the button, a clear bubble pops out of the box. It looks like a giant soap bubble, and after a few seconds it grows big enough to surround me.

Cool! I'm standing inside a bubble, and I can see everything clearly.

"I'd like a few other volunteers to test the bubble's strength," says Greg. "I have a straw and spitballs, a bow with rubber-tipped arrows, and in honor of the great Carl Bourette, an All Ball in the form of a baseball."

Emily, Abby, and Carl get up from their seats at the judges table and join us on stage.

"I'd be happy to fire an arrow at my brother," says Emily. She took archery at summer camp one year.

"And I can't think of anyone I'd rather shoot a spitball at!" adds Abby, her eyes twinkling mischievously.

"I guess you want me to throw that baseball, huh?" says Carl. "As long as you're positive that Billy won't get hurt."

"He won't. Not with the No-Trouble Bubble!" says Greg.

It's like he's already writing the commercial. This kid would definitely get along with Manny—who, I note, is the only judge not throwing anything at me.

Emily is first. She picks up the bow and fires an arrow right at me. I flinch. These rubber-tipped arrows usually stick to whatever they're aimed at. Not this one. Thankfully, it bounces right off the bubble and lands on the floor. *Whew!*

Next up is Abby. She chews a small piece of paper, then stuffs the slimy spitball into a straw. She fires it at me, and it's really hard not to duck this time too. But it also bounces right off the bubble without leaving even a drop of spit on the outside. This thing is AMAZING!

Carl picks up the baseball and tosses it from hand to hand. Even though I want to flinch, I'm secretly glad the All Ball isn't on its heavy BOWLING BALL setting. He raises his eyebrows, still apparently having some doubts about this.

"Go ahead, Carl," says Greg. "It'll be okay. Let 'er rip!"

"Let 'er rip!" I think. I know how hard Carl can throw. I've seen him throw out runners from deep in the hole at short. I don't think this is a very good—

Before I can finish my thought, I see Carl uncork a throw right at me. Pressing my palms against the sides of the bubble, I brace myself.

THWACK!

The baseball hits the bubble and bounces right back at Carl, who plucks it out of the air with his bare hand.

"And there you have it, ladies and gentlemen, boys and girls. The No-Trouble Bubble!" says Greg.

The audience cheers.

And that's when the bubble starts floating up into the air!

"Greg!" I shout. "Is it supposed to do this?"

"That's one of the little bugs I'd like your help working out," Greg shouts up to me.

Great idea, I think, I'd love to help you. If I ever get out of this thing! At the moment—up, up, UP!—I'm heading toward the ceiling! **Woosh!**

The stage crew rushes out with a very tall ladder. A stage hand climbs up quickly, grabs the bubble, and carries it back down to the stage. Now that I'm safely back on solid ground, I press the button again and the bubble vanishes.

"Sorry about that little glitch, Billy. Are you okay?"

Before I can answer, Manny steps up.

"Are you kidding?" he says to Greg. "That's no glitch, that's fantastic. Billy and I have been not only been trying to invent a Personal Force Field Belt, but we've been thinking about creating a hover device. I can see your invention ending up being the No-Trouble HOVER Bubble!"

That's Manny, already marketing a product we haven't even voted on yet!

"Thank you, Greg!" says Chris, as the judges all go back to our seats. "Well, those are our six finalists. How about a big hand for all of them, huh?"

The crowd claps. I look over my scores.

"Well, the big moment is almost here," says Chris. "The judges will tally their scores and decide the winner, which they share with all of us, right after these messages!"

Chapter Eleven

and the Winner Is . . .

AS WE GO TO COMMERCIAL, THE JUDGES HUDDLE together and discuss our scores.

"Well, I've got a clear winner," I say. "Despite that little, um, glitch, I think the No-Trouble Bubble is the way to go."

"I'm with you, partner," says Manny. "The No-Trouble Bubble is a no-brainer."

"Well, I think we may have a problem, gang," says Carl. "I think the Grow-With-You Shoes are the way to go. Don't forget, the Hyenas are going to endorse the winner. A shoe with the Hyenas' logo on it makes much

more sense than a bubble you can't even see. How are you gonna put a logo on that? How am I gonna come out and do a commercial for a clear bubble?"

All eyes turn to Emily.

"I'm with Carl," she says. "Those shoes are great. And they're ready to go. They could be in the stores in no time. I think they're a fantastic idea. *And* if we make them in heels, Dad will have to let me have some for my birthday."

Leave it to Emily. Her birthday is three weeks after mine, but she acts like it's three weeks before.

"I'm with the shoes too," says Abby. "I always have trouble finding shoes I like, or shoes that fit well. If I could buy one pair that looks good and fits well, and never think about buying shoes again, I'd be a happy camper."

"Who wants only one pair of shoes for their whole life?" I ask. "Wouldn't they wear out?"

"If they lasted through a kid's childhood, that would be plenty," Carl argues. "A kid who buys these will wear the Hyenas' logo for years and years. That works for me."

"Well, what do the scores tell us?" Manny asks.

Amazingly, when we do the math, the Grow-With-You Shoes and the No-Trouble Bubble have exactly the same total. It's an ABSOLUTE TIE.

"So what are you going to do, Billy?" asks Emily. "It's three judges against two."

That would mean the Grow-With-You Shoes should be the winner, but Manny and I *are* Sure Things, Inc. Shouldn't our votes count for more? After all, we'll be the ones actually putting out the invention. Before I can say another word, the stage manager steps out.

"And we're back from commercial in five . . . four . . . three . . . two . . . one!"

"Welcome back!" says Chris. "The judges have been tallying their scores and talking among themselves. Now the MOMENT WE'VE ALL BEEN WAITING FOR has arrived."

Chris turns and looks right at the judges' table. His voice turns deadly serious.

"Judges, do we have a winner?"

All the judges look at me.

What can I do?

"No," I say. "We don't."

The studio audience lets out a collective *gasp!*

"Still tallying the numbers, huh?" Chris says.

"No, we've added up our scores," I explain, "but we have a tie between two inventions and we can't come to an agreement."

Again the crowd gasps.

I see Chris give an off-camera hand signal to the stage manager.

"Well, this is certainly unexpected," he says, "but that's the excitement and drama of live TV, where you should always expect the unexpected! We're going to take another short break and we'll be back with your winner!"

"And . . . we're on break," says the stage manager.

Chris walks quickly to the judges' table.

"What's the problem?" he asks.

I quickly fill him in on our disagreement.

"Well, I love this drama, it's great for the ratings," he says, looking right at Manny and me. "But you boys did sign a contract stating that you would pick a clear winner and that Sure Things, Inc. would produce that winner's invention."

The look on Manny's face tells me all I need to know. He's imagining our first legal battle, draining all the company's profits. Not to mention what would happen to our reputation when word gets out that we didn't hold up our end of the agreement.

Leave it to my hero, Carl Bourette, to come to the RESCUE.

"Hang on, everybody," he says, standing up

and pulling out his phone. "I have an idea. Let me make a quick call."

"One minute to air!" shouts the stage manager.

I feel a knot form in my stomach as I stare at Carl talking quickly into his phone.

"Forty-five seconds!" shouts the stage manager.

The knot tightens. All Manny and I have worked for, all we have accomplished, might hinge on the outcome of this phone call.

"Thirty seconds!" calls the stage manager.

A big smile spreads across Carl's face. He slips his phone back into his pocket.

"Okay guys, we've got this covered," he says, sounding like he's about to make a play at second base. "I just spoke with the owner of the Hyenas, and she and I have agreed to personally invest in the Grow-With-You Shoes. The Hyenas logo will appear on the shoes, and I'll do the commercials, since I was going to do them anyway."

"Ten seconds!" shouts the stage manager.

"They won't be connected to Sure Things, Inc.," Carl continues, "but I think you boys will do okay without me. What do you think?"

"Five . . . four . . . three . . ."

"Deal!" Manny says, shaking Carl's hand. I couldn't agree more.

"Two . . . one . . . and we are back!"

This time there is no music, no spotlights, just Chris looking VERY SERIOUS.

"Well, folks, I have to tell you that we don't have a winner." He pauses to let this sink in. Then he breaks into a huge grin. "We have TWO winners!"

The audience goes wild. I can't be sure, but I think I see someone faint.

"Can Mallory and Greg please come back out onstage?"

The two winners rush out onto the stage. Mallory jumps up and down and gives Carl a big hug when he explains that the Hyenas will be endorsing the Grow-With-You Shoes. Her family joins her onstage, and they all have a group hug with Carl.

Manny and I shake hands with Greg.

"Sure Things, Inc. will fine-tune and release the No-Trouble Bubble," I say.

"I think we are going to have a hit on our hands," adds Manny.

"I am so excited to be working with you guys," says Greg. "I'm a huge fan."

"Why don't you come by the office tomorrow afternoon?" I suggest. "We can start right in on development."

"Fantastic!" cries Greg.

"This whole show has been exactly that— FANTASTIC!" says Chris, stepping up to join us. He addresses the audience and the viewers at home one last time. "Thanks for watching, and congratulations to both our winners. Good-bye, everybody!"

"And we're off!" shouts the stage manager.

"Thank you, guys," says Chris. "Nice save."

I walk over to Carl and shake his hand. "Saves are what you're best at," I say. "Thanks, Carl."

"No problem," Carl replies. "I think it's a real win-win. See ya round the ballpark."

• • •

That night, as I breathe a big sigh of relief and start to get excited about our next project, I shoot off an e-mail to Mom. I want to have another video chat with her. I can't wait to talk with her about how everything turned out. Exhausted, I climb into bed and quickly fall asleep.

The next morning, when I get up for school, I hurry to my computer. No reply from Mom. Hmm . . . she must be really busy. Maybe I'll hear from her later.

I practically sleepwalk through the school day. I'm still tired, but I am psyched about meeting with Greg at the office after school to start developing the No-Trouble Bubble.

After school I rush home, grab Philo, and head over to the office. Greg is already there.

"Hi, Billy. Manny has been showing me around," he says. "Your office is the COOL-EST PLACE I've ever seen. Especially your workbench. It's got everything you need to build great inventions."

"You sure you two aren't related?" Manny asks.

Philo comes sniffing around Greg's feet.

"Oh, this is Philo. He's here with us every day," I explain.

Greg scratches Philo's head, sending his tail whipping back and forth in overdrive. Then Philo trots over to his bed.

"So how do we start?" Greg asks.

"Let's see what you brought," I reply.

Greg empties his backpack onto my workbench. I open a drawer in my file cabinet and dig out the old blueprints I had drawn up for my Personal Force Field Belt idea. I never quite got it to work the way I wanted.

Greg opens up the control box on his No-Trouble Bubble prototype and looks over my blueprint.

"Interesting," he says, pointing at the paper. "I would never have thought of connecting those relays directly."

PERSONAL FORCE FIELD
— BELT —

Meanwhile, I study the inner workings of Greg's control box. "I think this circular pulse might be what caused the bubble to float," I say. "If we could build a regulator onto the box that would let the user control the hover feature, I think it would bring your invention to a WHOLE NEW LEVEL."

"Let's do it!" says Greg, opening up the toolbox he brought along.

"I never realized how much fun it is to work side-by-side with someone," I say, and as the words leave my mouth I cringe. Nice going, Billy. Way to make Manny feel unimportant. All I can hope is that my big idea to have Manny's favorite business magazine do a feature on him comes about. I'm close to finalizing the details, but I can't tell Manny about it just yet.

I turn toward Manny, but he's not looking at me and Greg. He's doing what he does best—mapping out a marketing plan for the No-Trouble Bubble.

A short while later we're ready to test the revised version.

"I think you should do the honors, Billy," says Greg.

Just as I'm about to press the button, the door to the office swings open, and in strolls Emily.

"I wanted to see how you guys are doing," she says. She slips off her backpack. "And it looks like I'm just in time to test the No-Trouble Bubble. I brought along a few things to help. After all, any chance to throw stuff at my brother . . ."

Emily opens her backpack and pulls out a football, a Frisbee, a small can of paint, and a slingshot.

"I hope this works," I say looking over Emily's arsenal.

The control box now has two knobs. One creates the bubble, the second—hopefully—controls the hover function.

I turn the first knob. Out pops a clear bubble that surrounds me. Emily wastes no time pelting me with projectiles. Each one bounces off the bubble harmlessly. Even the paint doesn't stick. The football flies past and lands near Manny's feet. Last, Emily tries the Sibling Silencer on me. But not even the Sibling Silencer can penetrate the bubble. In fact, the beam bounces right off the bubble and silences *her* instead!

Then Philo gets into the act, jumping onto the bubble and pawing at it before jumping off.

"Okay, here we go," I say. "Time to try the hover feature. Ready for takeoff." I twist the second knob and float into the air. As soon as I'm hovering—I'M FLYING! I'M REALLY FLYING!—I try using the commands to steer myself. But no such luck.

I drift out of control toward the ceiling. I'm going fast! **Woosh!** I try to wiggle around in the bubble, hoping the movements will bring me down, but they don't. I'm officially stuck!

Manny runs to get his dad, who not only is tall, but also has a ladder. He rushes up like a fireman and grabs me from the ceiling.

"Maybe you should take some sandbags with you, like on hot air balloons, just in case," he suggests. I nod glumly. I'm not sure how we're going to get this to work.

"Thanks for the entertainment," says Emily, who has regained her voice. "I'll leave you three GENIUSES to work out the bugs. Bye."

Oh sure! Show up, throw stuff at me, and leave. Nice. Real nice.

Greg and I open the control box and go back to work. A few minutes later we're ready to try again.

This time Manny spins his chair around.

"Maybe we should hold off on the hover feature," Manny says. "This product already works great, and we don't want to overdo it.

Besides, we can work on a hovercraft later. And Greg, we'll ask you to help out when we do."

Greg and I nod. I let out a huge sigh of relief. I'm just happy not to be an out-of-control floating guinea pig anymore. The No-Trouble Bubble helps you avoid trouble just like a Personal Force Field Belt would. And that is already way cool.

Chapter Twelve

Happy Birthday to Me?

I HEAD HOME, RIDING HIGH, THINKING ABOUT HOW cool the No-Trouble Bubble is going to be, but my good mood quickly vanishes. There's still no e-mail waiting for me from Mom.

Nothing. Not a word. And that's when the following thought pops into my mind:

Tomorrow is my BIRTHDAY!

In all the excitement with the TV show I hadn't really thought about my birthday for a few days. And now, here it is. Manny hasn't said a word about it. Neither has Dad or Emily. Or Mom, wherever she is.

My thirteenth birthday! The day I become a teenager. I mean, isn't that supposed to be a big deal?

I spend my last night as a twelve-year-old tossing and turning, jumping out of bed every half hour to check my e-mail to see if Mom has written back.

Nothing. All night.

When the big morning finally arrives, Dad still doesn't say anything as he makes breakfast, and Emily just looks at me strangely between bites of cereal. I'd think something was up with her, but it's Emily, so who knows what's going on in her brain? I head off to school, wondering if this is about to be the WORST BIRTHDAY of my life. I'm probably going to end up at home later, sitting alone in my room, not doing anything special at all. And I won't even hear from Mom.

I muddle through my school day. Again, no one says a word about my birthday. Not even the members of the inventors club or Samantha Jenkins. These kids are huge fans of mine, but even they say nothing! Not even a simple "happy birthday!"

At the office that afternoon the misery continues.

"How's the marketing for the rollout of the No-Trouble Bubble going?" I ask Manny, hoping that if we engage in conversation, a "happy birthday" might just slip out.

"Mmmm...," Manny says, which I translate as "okay." But nowhere in that "Mmmm..." is there a hint of a "happy birthday."

After a particularly unproductive day at the office, I get ready to head home.

"See you tomorrow," I say to Manny as Philo and I head for the door.

"Hmmm...," replies Manny. On a typical day that would pass for: "Bye, and have a good night." But today it sounds like, well, like a plain old "Hmmm."

When I arrive at home, things go from bad to worse.

"I'm home," I call out.

No reply.

"Dad? Em?"

Still nothing.

Where could they be? And why would they leave me alone on my birthday?

I head to the kitchen, where I find a note from Dad:

> Had to run out. Just heat up the leftovers from yesterday's hamburger-anchovy deluxe. It's in the fridge.
> —Dad

This really is the worst birthday ever! Eating Dad's leftovers all by myself. And he didn't even say "happy birthday" in his note.

Briiiiiiing!

My personal pity party is interrupted by the loud ring of the phone. I grab it. It's Manny. He does not sound good. In fact, he sounds terrible.

"We got a BIG PROBLEM, partner," he says.

The panic in his voice is clear. I've never heard Manny sound like this—ever!

"What's going on?" I ask.

"We have a MAJOR EMERGENCY with the No-Trouble Bubble," Manny says, sounding even worse than he did a few seconds earlier. "I mean, the whole thing, Sure Things, Inc., everything is about to go away. You have to come back to the office right now. Like, *right . . . now!*"

Wow, now I'm scared. I'm worried about Manny, not to mention the future of Sure Things, Inc.

"I'm on my way." I hang up and pedal furiously toward the office, my mind racing.

What could have happened? Could our bubble have finally burst? Maybe Manny discovered a problem with the No-Trouble Bubble. Or maybe this is about Manny feeling jealous of all the attention I get. Maybe he wants to break up our partnership, to end Sure Things, Inc.?

Suddenly my lousy birthday seems like the least of my worries.

I skid to a stop in front of Manny's garage

and jump off my bike. With Philo at my side, I rush into the office.

It's empty.

"Manny?" I shout.

Nothing. Okay, now I'm really confused.

That's when I notice Philo sniffing around behind Manny's desk. He trots over to a closet and starts barking. *aruuuf! Ruff! Ruff!*

"What's the matter, boy?"

Suddenly, a whole bunch people pop up from behind desks and burst out of dark corners!

"SURPRISE! HAPPY BIRTHDAY, BILLY!"

My brain starts spinning as I realize what is going on. There's Manny, smiling and giggling, and there's Dad and Emily. I spot Abby and Greg, and a bunch of kids from the inventors club. Samantha Jenkins holds up a printout of her mother's newest article about me and smiles.

"Happy birthday, partner!" Manny says, laughing at what must be a pretty funny-looking expression on my face.

"Happy birthday, Billy!" Dad says, giving me a big hug.

"Your shocked expression," Emily notes. "It's a good look for you."

"Happy birthday, Billy," says Abby. "I can't believe I'm friends with a real teenager!"

"Do you guys always have this much fun?" asks Greg.

I laugh as all the pieces of this puzzle fall into place. "So, all the secret conversations and the whispering, the tight-lipped answers, they were all about planning this surprise party?"

As I see the nods, I feel all the stress leave my body and a great weight lift from my shoulders.

"Well, you sure fooled me," I say, as my

mind shifts from shock to happiness. "This is a really great surprise."

"It's about to get even better," says Manny.

He walks to the door leading to his house and throws it open. There, standing in the doorway, is MOM!

"Happy birthday, Billy!" she says, running into the office and giving me a big hug. "Manny got in touch with me and told me how badly you wanted me to be part of your birthday. I had to be here on the big day for my teenage son!"

"So that's why I didn't hear back from you," I say to Mom. "You were traveling so you could be here with me. Wow."

Reason #312 why Manny is my best friend! He can even accomplish the impossible!

I turn to Manny. "This is the best surprise I've ever gotten," I say. "Thanks. And speaking of surprises, I have one for you, partner. I set up an interview for you with *Talking Biz*."

"That's my favorite business magazine," says Manny.

"I know. And they're thrilled to be doing a feature profile on you."

Although, like me, Manny never seeks out the spotlight for himself, I can see that he's very happy about this.

"Enough talking," says Dad. "I brought all kinds of fantastic food. Let's eat."

I look over at Emily as everyone gathers around the spread Dad has laid out. She pulls her hand from her pocket and flashes me a glimpse of the salt shaker filled with Gross-to-Good Powder. I smile, nod, and notice that she is no longer wearing rings on every finger. I guess that "thing" is finished. I can hardly wait to see what her next "thing" will be.

When the party is in full swing, Mom pulls me aside.

"Step outside with me for a second," she says. "I want to talk with you about something. In private."

We head out to a quiet corner of Manny's backyard. Now my mind is really spinning. What could she possibly want to tell me that

she couldn't say in front of everyone else?

"Remember when I tried your Best Test to find out what I was best at?" Mom asks.

I nod.

"And the helmet said that I was best at keeping secrets?"

Again I nod, wondering where in the world this is going.

"Well, your Best Test was right. I *am* best at keeping secrets, and I've been keeping secrets from you. I'm sorry, Billy. Let me explain everything."

Mom pauses for a second.

"I really wanted to be here for your birthday, Billy," she continues. "But I'm also here for another reason. When I leave, I want you to come with me. But we're not going to a government research lab. I'm afraid that's not where I work. I'm a spy, Billy. And I need your help!"

Want more Billy Sure?
Sure you do!
Turn the page for a sneak peek
at the next book in the Billy Sure
Kid Entrepreneur series!

I'm Billy Sure. Up until a moment ago, I thought I was a normal kid with normal school-work and a normal dog and normal chores. I've never felt anything but normal—okay, except for the fact that I'm also a world-famous inventor, but even then, still normal. Or so I thought.

But I just received the four biggest surprises of my life, each one bigger than the last. And now I'm not sure if I ever was normal.

Let me explain.

I'm thirteen years old. Actually, I turned thirteen today. I'm also a seventh-grader at Fillmore Middle School, and I'm the world-famous inventor behind the company Sure Things, Inc. I'm not saying that to brag or anything. I really don't like people who brag or who talk about how great they are. But to be honest, I am proud of what I have accomplished, even though my whole world just got thrown upside down!

Together with my best friend and business partner, Manny Reyes, I run Sure Things, Inc.

Our company has invented a whole bunch of popular stuff, like the All Ball (a ball that can change into any kind of sports ball) and the No-Trouble Bubble. Manny and I share an office. Well, it's really his parents' garage, but we've converted it into what the rest of the universe knows as the World Headquarters of Sure Things, Inc.

Anyway, a short while ago I arrived at the office after getting a panicked phone call from Manny. We had just finished judging a live TV special during which we picked Sure Things, Inc.'s next product, or as we like to call it, the Next Big Thing.

On the TV special, we selected an invention called the No-Trouble Bubble, a personal force field that can protect you from just about anything.

Two days after the show aired, Manny called me at home. He sounded super upset! He said that we have a problem with the No-Trouble Bubble that could result in the end of Sure Things, Inc.

Now that, as you can imagine, is pretty serious stuff. So I raced over to the office, hurried through the door, and, what do you know—I walked right SMACK! into a surprise party for my thirteenth birthday!

Surprise number one.

As it turns out, Manny's whole "we're in trouble" thing was a just ruse to get me over to the office, where my friends and family were waiting. My family being my dad, Bryan Sure, and Emily, my soon to be fifteen-year-old sister, who is, well . . . an older sister.

Usually my mom would be in that group too, but she's been away from home for a while. She works all over the world, and most of the time we have no idea where she is. She's a research scientist, or so she has always told me. In the weeks leading up to my big birthday (after all, you only become a teenager once), I had practically begged her to visit, but Mom kept saying that she couldn't make it.

Except she *could* make it. When Manny opened another door, I found out that Mom was:

Surprise number two!

But then, a few minutes after Mom's unexpected appearance, she asked me to step away from the party and go outside with her so we could talk about something "in private."

Naturally, my mind started racing. What could she want to talk about that is so important and so secret?

My mom revealed surprise number three. She's not really a research scientist. And nope, she hasn't been away in Antarctica like we thought. What I found out is something even cooler. My mom is a spy!

And then, immediately after, I received the fourth and by far the biggest surprise of all when Mom said to me:

"When I leave, I want you to come with me. I need your help."

So now? Now I'm stunned. I hardly know what to say. I stare at my mom in disbelief. Am I on the TV show *Prank Attack*, the one where they prank celebrities? I look closely at Mom's clothing. I peek around the backyard.

No hidden camera or microphone. No one is jumping out of the bushes.

This is real!

I'll be honest. Manny and I have thought my mom might be a spy for a while now. We've joked about it—especially a few months ago, after Mom sent me a "self-destructing" computer program to catch Alistair Swiped, a thief who was stealing my invention ideas. But then I remembered that Mom is just my mom. She's the kind of mom who orders in pizza and on more than one occasion laughed so hard that she spit all over my dad's shirt. The mom whose nickname for Philo is O-my-o Philo! Could that same Mom really be a spy?

"I know it's a lot to absorb, honey," Mom says. She looks around, as if she is half-expecting a team of top secret ninja spies to leap from the bushes and arrest her just for having this conversation with me. "You can ask me any questions you want."

My mind is reeling. A thousand questions

pop into my head, but I ask the most straight-forward one first.

"Who do you work for? The CIA? The FBI? The Secret Service?"

"I can't say," Mom says.

"You can tell me," I press.

"No, I really can't say," Mom replies. "I'm not trying to dodge your question, Billy, but if I tried to say the agency's name, my tongue would fall out." Then she looks kinda sad. "Poor Agent Lugman found out the hard way."

Is she for real?

"I'm thirteen," I say, coming to a realization. "That means you've been keeping this secret for thirteen years! Why tell me the truth now?"

"I am truly sorry, honey," she says, taking my hand. "It was just safer for the whole family if you and Emily didn't know. As to why now, well . . . I need your help. Specifically, your genius for inventing."